"How dare you speak to me like that?"

His voice was molten.

Camilla met his gaze. Eyes dark as obsidian, she thought with a strange clarity, and as hard as flint. But with a small flame burning....

Just as she was burning inside.

She drew a deep angry breath. "Because it wasn't me that you...seduced and abandoned in Athens. It was my sister, Katie." A sob rose in her throat. "And you can't even remember what she looks like."

SARA CRAVEN was born in South Devon, England, and grew up surrounded by books, in a house by the sea. After leaving grammar school she worked as a local journalist covering everything from flower shows to murders. She started writing for Harlequin Mills & Boon in 1975. Apart from writing, her passions include films, music, cooking and eating in good restaurants.

Books by Sara Craven

HARLEQUIN PRESENTS

Don't miss any of our special offers. Write to us at the following address for information on our newest releases.

Harlequin Reader Service
U.S.: 3010 Walden Ave., P.O. Box 1325, Buffalo, NY 14269
Canadian: P.O. Box 609, Fort Erie, Ont. L2A 5X3

Sara Craven
DARK APOLLO

Harlequin Books

TORONTO • NEW YORK • LONDON
AMSTERDAM • PARIS • SYDNEY • HAMBURG
STOCKHOLM • ATHENS • TOKYO • MILAN
MADRID • WARSAW • BUDAPEST • AUCKLAND

ISBN 0-373-11786-8

DARK APOLLO

First North American Publication 1996.

Copyright © 1994 by Sara Craven.

CHAPTER ONE

'But he loves me.'

'I wouldn't count on it.' Camilla Dryden spoke more brusquely than she'd intended, and repented instantly as she saw her sister's eyes cloud with bewildered hurt.

'Katie, love,' she went on more gently, 'you hardly know each other. It was a holiday romance. Just—one of those things.'

She could hardly believe her own ears. One cliché was following another, and she wasn't surprised to see Katie shaking her head.

'It wasn't like that. I knew as soon as I met Spiro that there would never be anyone else. And he feels just the same about me.'

Camilla winced inwardly. 'Then why wasn't he on that flight? Or any of today's other flights, for that matter?'

'I don't know. Something must have happened to prevent him—delay him.'

Camilla could make a cynical guess what that 'something' might be. Spiridion Xandreou had probably remembered, just in time, that he had a fiancée—or even a wife—already.

This is what comes, she thought seething, of allowing an impressionable eighteen-year-old to spend Easter in Greece.

It had seemed a perfectly acceptable invitation at the time. Lorna Stephens, Katie's best friend, was going to Athens to visit her aunt, married to a Greek businessman. The two girls had been working hard for their public examinations, and deserved a break from their studies.

How could Camilla have guessed that Lorna's aunt was the kind of irresponsible idiot who'd allow her niece and her niece's friend to be chatted up by personable Greek waiters?

If only it had stopped at chat, Camilla thought with a silent groan. Or if Katie had been sophisticated enough to realise she was being spun a line by an experienced charmer.

On her return, she'd informed her elder sister that, although she was still prepared to take her A levels, they no longer mattered because she was engaged to be married.

Camilla had taken a deep, steadying breath, and done some gentle probing.

What had emerged was hardly reassuring. Spiro, it seemed, worked in a marvellous and famous restaurant where Katie had gone for a meal with the family party. Spiro had served at their table, and the following evening Katie and Lorna had managed to return to the restaurant alone.

'Of course, he's not really just a waiter.' Katie's eyes had been full of stars, and a new womanly awareness which had struck a chill to Camilla's heart. 'His family own the restaurant, and masses of other things beside—

hotels, even a shipping line. From what Spiro says, they must be amazingly wealthy. Isn't it incredible?'

'It certainly is,' Camilla had agreed, but Katie had been oblivious to the irony in her voice.

'When my exams are over, Spiro's flying over to meet you, and ask formally if he can marry me.' She had smiled tenderly. 'He's very old-fashioned.'

Well, he'd certainly chosen the right route to Katie's heart, Camilla had thought savagely. Katie was old-fashioned too, a shy, gentle girl, who before that Athenian spring had had her heart set on university and an academic career. First love should have come gently to her too, not force-fed under a Greek sun by some plausible Lothario.

She'd thought, She's going to be so hurt.

But, to her surprise, letters with Greek stamps had begun to arrive regularly and frequently.

Perhaps Spiro Xandreou knew Lorna's rich uncle, and assumed Katie came from the same kind of background.

Little does he know, she'd thought, looking round their small flat. When he realised that Katie's only relative was an older sister working for a busy secretarial agency to keep a roof over their heads, this so-called engagement would be a thing of the past.

Camilla had never been to Greece, but she had a shrewd idea that marriages there were still very much tied up with property, and the size of a bride's potential dowry. Katie had no financial qualification to recommend her to the family of a young waiter on the make.

For a time, it had seemed as if Katie was having second thoughts about her romance as well. She had been silent and preoccupied, and spent a lot of time alone in her room. She'd lost weight too, and there were shadows under her eyes.

But then another letter arrived, and Katie, bubbling with renewed happiness, had revealed that Spiro was flying to London at the end of June.

But his flight had landed without him, and Katie had eventually returned to the flat alone, almost distraught with worry.

And now Camilla had to make her see reason.

'Surely he'd have sent word if he'd been delayed,' she said. 'I think,' she added carefully, 'we're going to have to accept, darling, that he's simply changed his mind...'

'He can't have done.' Bright spots of colour burned in Katie's cheeks. 'We're going to be married. He—he has to come here. Oh, Camilla, he's simply got to.'

Camilla looked at her in sudden horrified understanding. She didn't have to ask why, she thought. It was all there in Katie's tear-bright eyes and trembling mouth, in the curious blend of dignity and shame in her face as she looked back at her sister.

Her voice broke. 'Oh, no, Katie. For God's sake—not that.'

'It's quite true. I'm going to have Spiro's baby. But it's all right, because he loves me, and we're going to be married as soon as it can be arranged.'

Camilla's voice was weary. 'You've actually told him you're pregnant?' She gave a mirthless smile. 'And you wonder why he wasn't on that plane.'

'You're not to say that.' Katie's voice shook with intensity. 'You don't know him. He's decent and honourable.'

'So decent, so honourable he couldn't wait to seduce a girl on her first trip abroad.' Camilla shook her head, her throat aching with grief and bitterness. 'Oh, Katie, you fool.' She sighed. 'Well, now we have to decide what to do for the best.'

'I know what you're going to say.' Katie's face was suddenly pale. 'Don't even think it, Milla. I'm having this baby.'

'Darling, you haven't thought it through. You've got your university course—your whole life ahead of you. You can't imagine what it would be like trying to cope with a baby as well...'

'But that isn't what I've chosen. I'm going to marry Spiro. It isn't the life I'd planned, I agree, but it's the life I want—the only one, now and forever.'

'Katie—you can't know that.'

'Mother knew it, when she met Father. And she was younger than me,' Katie said unanswerably. 'And you can't say they weren't happy.'

No, Camilla thought. She couldn't say that. Her parents had loved each other deeply and joyously until a jack-knifing lorry had brought that love to a premature end, leaving her at nineteen with the sole responsibility for a vulnerable adolescent.

And what a hash I've made of it, she castigated herself. She needed her mother's wisdom to tell her how to support Katie through this crisis. I don't know what to do, she thought, and felt a hundred years old.

She felt even older when she woke the next morning. It had been a terrible evening. Katie had managed to telephone the restaurant in Athens, only to be told with polite but impersonal regret that Spiro no longer worked there. Nor could they say where he'd gone.

I bet they can't, Camilla had thought, seething. They're probably inundated with calls like this.

All night long, Camilla had heard the sound of Katie's desolate sobbing through the thin partition wall. She'd tried to go to her, but Katie's door was locked. Besides, what could she do, or say—she who had never been even marginally tempted to fall in love herself? She was the last person in the world to know what comfort or advice to offer, she'd told herself unhappily.

To her surprise she found Katie already up, and making breakfast in the tiny kitchenette. Her sister looked wan and red-eyed, but her face was set with determination.

'I'm going to find him, Milla,' she said.

'But you can't trail round every restaurant and taverna in Athens asking for him. It would be like searching for a needle in a haystack.' Dismayed, Camilla took the beaker of coffee Katie handed her.

'Not Athens.' Katie shook her head. 'Spiro comes from an island called Karthos. It's in the Ionian Sea, south of Corfu. I shall go there. His family must know where he is.'

Camilla took a wary sip of the strong black brew. 'Katie,' she said hesitantly, 'has it occurred to you that Spiro may not—want to be found?'

'That's not true,' Katie said calmly. 'If it were, I'd know it here.' She put her hand on her heart.

The simplicity of the gesture and the profound trust it implied made Camilla's throat ache with unshed tears.

He's not worth it, she thought savagely.

There were a thousand arguments she ought to be able to use to stop Katie embarking on this crazy and probably fruitless quest, but somehow she couldn't think of one.

Instead, she said, 'Then I'm going with you.'

'Milla, do you mean it?' Katie's face was transfigured. 'But what about the agency? Will Mrs Strathmore give you the time off?'

'I've a whole backlog of leave I haven't taken.' Camilla gave her a reassuring smile. 'And Mrs Strathmore can lump it. She won't sack me. She relies on me to handle the ghastly clients the others won't work for. I'll call in and explain on the way round to the travel agency.' She tried to sound positive and encouraging, but her heart was in her boots.

What the hell will we do if we don't find him? she wondered. Or, even worse, supposing we find him and he doesn't want to know?

She sighed silently. They would cross that bridge when they came to it.

'We'll find him.' Katie seemed to have read her thoughts. Her voice and face were serene. 'It's fate. The Greeks have always believed in fate.'

And in the Furies, Camilla thought grimly. The so-called Kindly Ones inexorably pursuing the erring, and wreaking their vengeance on them.

Well, she would be a latter-day Fury, trailing Spiro Xandreou, no matter how well he might have covered his tracks.

She said, 'There's no such thing as fate,' and surreptitiously crossed her fingers under the kitchen table.

*   *   *

The Hotel Dionysius was small, fiercely clean, and frankly basic. Camilla sat at a plastic-covered table in a corner of the outside restaurant area, a tall glass of freshly squeezed orange juice in front of her. She was sheltered from the glare of the midday sun by a thatched roof, interwoven with a sprawling and healthy vine. Beyond the hotel's tiny garden with its hibiscus hedge lay the main square of Karthos town.

The island was only a remote dot in the Ionian Sea, but it was bustling with tourists. So far Camilla had heard French, German and Dutch being spoken, as well as English, and she and Katie had been lucky to get the last two vacancies at the hotel.

She'd left Katie sleeping in their whitewashed shuttered room on the first floor. She was beginning to feel the effects of her pregnancy, and had been miserably sick on the flight to Zakynthos, and the subsequent long ferry trip. The temperature on Karthos was already up in the eighties, and she'd agreed with little fuss to Camilla's suggestion that she should rest and leave the initial enquiries for Spiro to her sister.

Camilla had been sorely tempted to cancel this whole wild-goose chase after a reluctant telephone call to Lorna Stephens' Greek uncle. She'd explained, without going into detail, that she was anxious to trace a young waiter from the restaurant Clio, and wondered if he could help.

To judge by the cynical sigh, and muttered, '*Po, po, po,*' no further explanation was needed. 'You know the name of this man, *thespinis*?'

'He's called Spiro Xandreou.'

'Xandreou?' Across the miles, she heard the sharp intake of breath. Then, 'I regret I cannot assist you. But I advise you most strongly, *thespinis*, to proceed no further in this.' A pause. 'Most strongly.' And he'd rung off, leaving Camilla with a host of unanswered questions.

She'd been warned off, she realised uneasily. She could only hope that Spiro wasn't some kind of thug—a member of the Greek mafia, if there was such a thing. Maybe he wasn't on Karthos at all, but in gaol somewhere.

But how could she tell Katie her suspicions, and burst the bubble of optimism and anticipation which encircled her? Maybe she just had to let her find out for herself, she concluded resignedly.

Camilla sighed silently as she finished the iced fruit juice.

But where on earth should their search start?

'You enjoy?' Kostas, the hotel's burly proprietor, arrived to clear the table. He had a thick black moustache, a booming laugh, and he smoked incessantly. But the warmth of his welcome had been quite unfeigned, and to Camilla's relief he spoke better than rudimentary English. The questions she needed to ask were omitted from the usual phrase books.

She nodded vigorously. 'It was delicious, thank you. Just what I needed.'

'To travel in this heat is not good.'

As he turned away, she said, 'Kostas, do you know a family called Xandreou—with a son named Spiro?'

The genial smile vanished as if it had been wiped away. He looked startled, and almost apprehensive. 'Why do you ask?'

She said lightly, 'Oh, our families used to be—acquainted. I believe they come from here, and I'd like to see them again. That's all.'

There was a silence, then, 'Xandreou, you say?' Kostas shook his head. 'I don't know the name. You have come to the wrong place, I think, *thespinis*.'

'I don't think so.' She gave him a level look. 'You're sure you haven't heard of them?'

'Certain.' He paused. 'You are on holiday, *thespinis*. You should relax. Go to the beach— enjoy the sun—drink some wine. Make other friends—and don't waste time looking for these people.'

And if that wasn't an oblique warning, she'd never heard one, Camilla thought, watching him walk away between the tables, which were already filling up for lunch.

It was the same message she'd got from Athens: keep away from the Xandreou clan.

Everyone knows them, but they don't want to talk about them, she thought, a prickle of wariness running down her spine. Yet,

somehow, for Katie's sake, she had to pen-
etrate this wall of silence.

She picked up her bag, and walked to the
steep outside stairway which provided an
alternative access to the bedrooms.

There'd been some cards on the reception
desk advertising car and motorbike hire. She'd
rent a scooter and take a preliminary look
round. The brochure on the island had warned
that most of the best beaches were out of town,
and it might be pleasant to find some deserted
cove and laze around for a while before the real
business of their trip began.

'Journeys end in lovers meeting', she
thought. I only hope it's true.

She was halfway up the steep outside
staircase that provided an alternative access to
the bedrooms when a voice below her said urgently, '*Thespinis.*'

Glancing down, she saw one of the hotel
waiters, who'd been serving an adjoining table
while she spoke to Kostas. He gave her an in-
gratiating smile. 'You want Spiro Xandreou?'

'Why, yes.' Her heartbeat quickened in swift
excitement. 'Do you know him?'

'Since boys.' He touched a fist theatrically
to his chest. 'I too am a man of Karthos.'

'Then can you tell me where to find him?'

The young man shrugged, sending a slightly
furtive glance back over his shoulder. 'Is not
easy for me, you understand...'

Camilla understood perfectly. She extracted a thousand-drachma note from her wallet, and handed it over.

He whispered hoarsely, 'He is at his house— the Villa Apollo.'

'Is that near here?'

'*Ochi*.' He gestured towards the craggy hills which formed the island's hinterland. 'Is long way.'

'Is there a bus?'

'No bus. Nothing there—only villa. You get car, or motorbike.' He handed her one of the cards displayed in Reception. 'My cousin rent—very cheap.'

With you on commission, no doubt, she returned silently. But she thanked him politely, and went on up the steps.

'*Thespinis*,' he hissed again, and she paused. '*Thespinis*, whatever occur, you don't say to boss I told you, *ne*?'

'Not a word,' she said, and watched him vanish into the hotel.

Katie was still out for the count. Camilla wrote her a brief note saying she was going to explore, and replaced the simple button-through dress she'd worn for the journey with white shorts and a sleeveless top, with her initial in red and gold embroidery over the left breast. She gathered her thick chestnut hair into a barrette at the nape of her neck for coolness, and slid her feet into comfortable canvas shoes.

She found the rental place easily enough. It was basically a dirt yard, with chickens pecking round between the scooters. Andonis, the owner, wore a grubby singlet and a three-day growth, and had the kind of gleam in his eye which made Camilla regret she hadn't changed into something less revealing.

She was able to hire a scooter with a disturbing lack of formality, although the actual cost was rather more than she'd bargained for. She enquired about a safety helmet, and Andonis stared at her as if she were mad, then spat on the ground.

'Karthos roads are good,' he said flatly. Her request for a map of the island met with more luck, however. A photocopied sheet, dog-eared and much folded, was produced.

Camilla stared at the web of roads, wondering where she would find the spider.

'I'm looking for a particular house—the Villa Apollo,' she said. 'Can you mark it for me?'

He whistled through the gap in his teeth. 'You want Xandreou?' He gave her another lascivious look. 'So do many women. He's lucky man.'

Well, his luck's about to change, Camilla thought grimly. Andonis's remark, and the grin that accompanied it, had only confirmed all her worst fears. Katie's honourable lover was nothing more than a practised Casanova, she realised with disgust.

Andonis made a laborious pencil cross on the map. 'Villa Apollo,' he said. He gave her another openly appraising stare. 'You should tell me before. Maybe I make special price for Xandreou's woman.'

Presumably they arrived in convoys, Camilla thought with distaste.

She distanced Andonis, who was disposed to help her on to the scooter, with an icy look.

'You're mistaken, *kyrie*. I'm not—what you say.'

The grin widened, unabashed. He shrugged. 'Not now, maybe, but who knows?'

'I do,' Camilla said curtly, and rode off.

This was obviously what they'd all been trying to warn her about, she thought, as she headed out of town on the road Andonis had indicated.

Innocent Katie had given her heart and her body to a worthless piece of womanising scum. Well, he wasn't going to get away with it.

'Xandreou's woman', she thought with contempt. What a tag to be branded with.

But I'll make him pay for it, she vowed under her breath, if it's the last thing I do.

'Whatever occur'. The waiter's words sneaked unexpectedly back into her mind.

An odd thing to say, she thought. Almost like another warning. And, in spite of the intense heat, she felt suddenly, strangely cold.

CHAPTER TWO

CAMILLA brought the scooter gingerly to a halt on the stony verge, and wiped the sweat from her forehead.

Much further, and she would run out of road. Already the surface had dwindled to the status of a track, yet there was still no sign of the Villa Apollo. Had Andonis deliberately sent her to a dead end?

She eased the base of her spine with a faint grimace. He'd certainly given her the maverick of his scooter collection. The steering had a mind of its own, and the brakes barely existed. If she had to do an emergency stop...

Not that there seemed much chance of that. So far she hadn't passed another living thing, except for a donkey, a couple of tethered goats, and a dog on a chain who'd barked at her.

The road, rising steeply, was lined on each side with olive groves, and their silvery canopy had protected her from the worst of the sun. Some of the trees, with their gnarled and twisted trunks, seemed incredibly old, but they were still bearing fruit. The netting spread on the ground beneath to catch the olives bore witness to that.

Camilla turned and looked behind her, as if to remind herself that civilisation did exist.

Below her, in the distance, glimpsed in the gaps between the clustering olives, were the multi-coloured roofs and white walls of Karthos town, topped by the vivid blue dome of a church. And beyond that again, azure, jade and amethyst, was the sea.

I could be on a beach now, she thought wistfully, if I weren't riding this two-wheeled death-trap up the side of a mountain.

She sighed, as she eased the clinging top away from the damp heat of her body, imagining herself sliding down from some convenient rock into cool, deep water, salty and cleansing against her skin.

One more bend in the road, she told herself. Then I go back.

She coaxed the scooter back to life, and set off, trying to correct its ferocious wobble on corners. In doing so, she nearly missed the Villa Apollo altogether.

She came to a halt, dirt and gravel flying under the tyres, and stared at the letters carved into the two stone gateposts ahead of her. And beneath them the emblem of the sun—the sign of the god Apollo himself, who each day, according to legend, drove his fiery chariot through the heavens.

Camilla dismounted with care, propping her machine against the rocky bank. With luck, someone terminally insane with a death wish might just steal it.

Beyond the gateway, more olive trees shadowed a steeply lifting driveway.

Right, she thought, tilting her chin. Let's see this irresistible Adonis who causes such havoc in people's lives. Hands in pockets, she set off up the gradient, moving with a brisk, confident stride that totally masked her inner unease. Knowing she had right on her side did little to calm her nerves, she discovered.

And when the man stepped out in front of her, she only just managed to stifle a yell of sheer fright.

One glance told her that he wasn't the one she'd come to find. He was stocky and grizzled, with a walkie-talkie in his hand, and a gun, she noted, swallowing, in a holster on his hip. His face was unwelcoming, his stance aggressive as he barked a question at her in Greek.

Camilla stood her ground. 'I don't understand,' she said. 'My name is Dryden, and I have come from England to see Mr Xandreou.'

An armed security man, she thought. What am I getting into here?

The man stared at her for a moment, then spoke into his radio. He listened, then jerked his head at Camilla, indicating that she should follow.

The drive curved away to the right and Camilla saw that the olives gave way to lawns of coarse grass, and flowerbeds bright with colour.

And beyond them was the house itself, the Villa Apollo, large and sprawling, its white walls dazzling in the sunshine. It was surrounded by a colonnaded terrace, festooned in purple and crimson bougainvillaea, and a smoky pink flowering vine.

Camilla slowed, staring round her. What did a waiter in an Athens restaurant have to do with this frankly glamorous background? she asked herself. Unless Spiro Xandreou was merely an employee, and she was being shown to the tradesman's entrance.

The security man looked back, gesturing impatiently, and she moved forward reluctantly. Ahead of her, she saw the clear turquoise sparkle of a large swimming-pool. Around the edge were tiles in an intricate mosaic pattern, and loungers and chairs stood waiting under fringed sun umbrellas. There was a table with a tray of drinks, and on the edge of the pool a twin of the radio device carried by the security man.

Otherwise, the place seemed deserted.

As she stared round her in bewilderment, a man's dark head suddenly broke the surface of the water. Camilla felt her heart beating slowly and unevenly as he pulled himself athletically from the pool, and stood for a moment, shaking the excess water from his mane of black curling hair.

He was well above average height, she saw, broad-shouldered and narrow-hipped, his bronzed body lean, muscular and perfectly proportioned.

He was good-looking too, she recognised dazedly, his almost classical beauty of feature redeemed by the inherent toughness and strength of his mouth and chin. A man to be reckoned with.

'Like a Greek god.' She'd heard the phrase many times, but never expected to see it brought to life in front of her.

Especially as, like most of the ancient classical statues of the Olympians and heroes, he was completely naked.

Moving with the lithe grace of a jungle animal, he walked over to one of the loungers, picked up a waiting towel, and began to dry himself, casually and without haste, ignoring the presence of the new arrivals.

Camilla knew that displaying himself like this in front of her—a woman, and a stranger—was a calculated insult. But if he expected her to blush or faint, or run off screaming like some frightened nymph from mythology, he'd be disappointed, she told herself, and stood waiting in stony silence, refusing to let the deliberate affront get to her.

Eventually, he draped the damp towel round his hips, securing it with a knot. He reached for the thin, elegant platinum watch on the table, and clasped the bracelet on to his wrist, allowing his gaze, at last, to rest coolly and dispassionately on Camilla. His eyes were dark, long-lashed, holding an odd glitter.

Like cold fire, she thought.

He said, 'Who are you, and what do you want here?'

His voice was low and drawling, the accent only slightly marked. But then Katie had told her his English was excellent.

Katie, she thought with a kind of despair. No wonder she'd fallen for him hook, line and sinker. But why should a sophisticated man of the world like this have encouraged her inexperienced sister, even for a moment? It made no sense at all. Unless he still wasn't the one she sought.

'Well?' His voice prodded at her impatiently. 'You have forced your way in here. Why don't you speak?'

She said slowly, gauging his reaction, 'I want to talk about—Xandreou's woman.'

He filled a glass with mineral water from one of the bottles, and drank. The security man, she realised, had discreetly faded away.

He said, 'I think you flatter yourself, Kyria . . . ?'

'Dryden,' she supplied again. 'Please don't pretend you've forgotten the name.'

He shrugged. 'It is vaguely familiar.' He sounded bored. The brilliant eyes went over her, lingering on her breasts and thighs and long, slim legs, making her uneasily aware that the heat had made her scanty garments into a second skin.

His gaze met hers again. 'So, what do you want, Kyria Dryden? Or do you plan to spend the whole afternoon staring at me in silence?'

'I'm sorry.' What am I apologising for? she asked herself in disbelief. She pulled herself together with determination. 'You aren't exactly what I expected, Kyrios Xandreou.'

'Nor are you. But it isn't important.' His tone was dismissive. 'Say what you must, and go.'

All her worst forebodings were confirmed. He didn't care about Katie, or the baby. Her sister's sole attraction for him had been her innocence. Now it was gone, he didn't want to know. Katie was just another notch on a well-dented bedpost.

She said stonily. 'You know why I'm here. I think some kind of—reparation is called for.'

'For what? A pleasant interlude like so many of your countrywomen expect to enjoy in Greece?' The contempt in his voice lashed her.

Just because other girls might behave like sex-crazed idiots, there was no need to tar Katie with the same brush, she thought in furious anguish. Hadn't he realised that she was different—that she'd actually believed whatever corny seduction line he'd handed her?

'Unfortunately, this particular interlude has had consequences.' She hated the smile which twisted his mouth. 'Or had you forgotten there's a baby on the way?'

'There is nothing wrong with my memory,' he said. 'It is more a question of credulity, perhaps. A child with Xandreou blood might have a claim on Xandreou money. Is that what you think?' He shook his head. 'I am not a fool, Kyria Dryden. I am prepared to subject the paternity of this child to every test available to medical science. But can you afford to fight me?' The studied insolence of his gaze scorched her again. 'I don't think so.'

'No,' she said curtly. 'Nor would I dream of it. Obviously your responsibilities mean very little to you.'

'You are wrong. They mean a great deal. Which is why I will not submit to pressure from a girl who has behaved like a slut, and now wishes to benefit from her indiscretion.' His drawl intensified. 'Perhaps you are not aware that in Greek the name Catherine means "purity". It is something to consider—for the future, *ne*?'

Her hands curled into fists at her sides, and her voice shook a little.

'You've more than made your point, Mr Xandreou. I'd hoped you might have some shred of decency in you, but clearly I was mistaken. However, you won't be troubled again. The baby may not be brought up in the lap of this kind of luxury——' she gestured scornfully round her '—but it will be welcomed, looked after and loved, and that's far more important. It wasn't money I came for, but something more fundamental. Something you wouldn't understand.'

She paused, struggling to control her voice. 'And, hopefully, although the baby will be illegitimate, it will grow up without knowing what a complete bastard its father was.' She drew a deep and shuddering breath. 'I wonder how many more lives will be ruined before you get your well-deserved come-uppance?'

'You have the insolence to talk about ruined lives?' He flung his head back, and she felt his anger touch her like a blast of lightning. 'How dare you say such a thing—speak to me like this?'

'It's quite simple,' she said. 'I just tell the truth.'

She turned and walked away from him, back rigidly straight, fighting the storm of angry tears which threatened to overwhelm her.

Of all the hateful, disgusting things he'd said, it was the gibe about Katie's name which, ridiculously, had got to her most.

He must have known she was untouched, yet he'd set out deliberately to deflower and destroy, using all the potent virility and sexual charisma he possessed in such abundance to undermine her resistance.

My God, I was aware of it myself, she thought, shame mingling with anger. And I was only with him for a few minutes. If I'd met him in different circumstances—if he'd been charming, or even marginally polite...

She blotted out that line of thinking instantly. Spiro Xandreou clearly regarded himself as some latter-day Apollo, a sun god to whom every woman was a potential victim for conquest, and she disgraced herself by even acknowledging his attraction.

But what had he been doing, working in that restaurant? she asked herself. Waiting on tables for a bet—or some other kind of sick joke?

If so, why go on with the pretence once Katie had returned to England? Promising to come over—claiming they were going to be married. All those letters—all those lies.

Unforgivable, she thought as she dragged the despised scooter upright, and kicked it into grumbling life. She wanted to get away from the Villa Apollo, and its owner, as fast as she could—breathe some untainted air.

And decide what she could possibly tell Katie, she thought despondently as she steadied her temperamental machine for the first bend.

The open-topped sports car was upon her instantly, racing up the hill on the wrong side of the road. Camilla caught a stunned glimpse of a girl's face, olive-skinned and pretty behind the designer sunglasses but transfixed by sheer horror. Then she pulled the bike over in a kind of desperation, striving to avoid the inevitable collision.

The scooter hit the loose stones on the verge, and went out of control, running up the bank. Camilla was thrown off, landing painfully on her side. She lay still for a moment, feeling sick and dizzy with shock.

She heard the sound of running feet, and the girl bent over her. '*O Theos.*' There was panic in her voice. 'You are hurt. Are you broken anywhere?'

Into several pieces by the feel of it, Camilla thought, as she pulled herself to her feet. There were no actual fractures, she was sure, but there was a deep graze on her bare leg, and another on her arm, blood mingling with the dirt on her torn blouse.

'I did not expect anyone else on this road.' The girl was practically wringing her hands.

'So I gathered,' Camilla forced from her dry throat.

'You need a doctor.' The girl took her un-injured arm, urging her towards the car. 'With me, please. Come.'

Camilla shook her head. 'It's all right.' Her voice sounded very small and far-away suddenly. 'I—I'll be fine.' She saw the road, the car, and the newcomer's anxious face dip and sway, then everything descended into a dark and swirling void.

Somewhere, a storm must be raging. Camilla could feel the splash of rain on her face and hear a distant rumble of thunder. But she herself seemed to be floating on some kind of cloud.

She opened unwilling eyes, and stared up at a face she'd never seen before, female, elderly and wrinkled with concern. Nor was it raining. She was simply having her face bathed with cool water.

I hurt, she thought, wincing, as she looked around her. She was in a large room, lying on a vast luxurious sofa the colour of rich maize.

And the sound of the storm was Spiro Xandreou, who was standing a few feet away conducting a low-voiced but furious argument with the girl from the car.

Oh, my God, Camilla thought with horrified alarm. She's brought me back here—to his house. I can't bear it.

She tried to sit up, only to be vociferously restrained by the old woman attending to her.

Spiro Xandreou swung round, frowning, and came striding over. He'd exchanged the towel, Camilla noticed, for a pair of white shorts almost equally revealing. Still competing for the Stud of the Year award, no doubt, she thought, hating him.

'My sister has told me what happened,' he said harshly. 'You must remain where you are—keep still until the doctor has made his examination.'

'I'll do nothing of the kind.' Camilla's head swam as she put her feet gingerly to the floor. But she was becoming more aware of her surroundings. One entire wall of the room was made from glass, a series of sliding doors pushed open to admit the sunlight, and a breeze bringing a hint of flowers and citrus.

The floor was tiled in creamy marble, veined in blue and gold, and the same blue was echoed in the colour of the walls, which were bare except for a few modern abstract paintings, clearly original and probably valuable.

Ironically, the one thing Spiro Xandreou hadn't lied about was his wealth, Camilla thought sourly. She was in the lap of luxury here. The sofa she was lying on was one of a pair flanking a wide marble fireplace, which was presumably for use in the winter months but was now screened by a large bronze sculpture of a sunburst.

The whole effect was airy and spacious, yet somehow welcoming, so presumably the owner had had no hand in the décor.

She glared up at him. 'There's no need for all this fuss. I want nothing from you, Mr. Xandreou. I thought I'd made that clear.'

'Unfortunately, neither of us has a choice. You are not leaving here, *thespinis*, without medical attention.'

'What are you afraid of? That I'll sue?' His autocratic tone needled her. She tried to smile past him at the girl, who was standing looking sullen, her arms crossed defensively in front of her. 'I shan't. I've a few grazes, that's all.'

'You cannot know that. And in the circumstances we can afford to take no risks,' he said grimly. He issued some low-voiced instructions to the old woman who left the room instantly.

'Arianna tells me you were riding a scooter,' he went on. 'Are you quite crazy?'

'Only on a part-time basis,' Camilla said wearily. 'Look—just get me a taxi, and I'll go back to my hotel. My sister will be wondering where I am, and I don't want to cause her unnecessary worry,' she added pointedly.

'She knows of your activities, then—and she permitted them?' Spiro Xandreou raised clenched fists towards the ceiling. 'Unbelievable.'

'No,' Camilla said, with a sigh. 'This was all my own idea. And clearly a bad one.'

'At least we agree on something,' he said silkily.

The old woman in her black dress and snowy apron came back into the room, carrying a bowl of steaming water, a bottle of antiseptic, and some cotton wool.

Camilla eyed them with misgiving. 'There's no need ...'

'There is every need,' he contradicted flatly. 'This is not England, Kyria Dryden. Grazes such as this carry a risk of infection, and need immediate attention.'

He knelt beside the sofa, his face coolly intent, soaking a swab of cotton wool in the antiseptic solution.

Camilla wanted to draw away. He was altogether too close for comfort, she thought, dry-mouthed, as she absorbed the clean, fresh scent of his sun-warmed skin. His bare shoulder brushed against her knee, and she felt a sharp pang deep inside her that had nothing to do with pain.

She said huskily, 'No—please ...'

He gave her a look of withering contempt and began to swab the dirt and grains of gravel from her leg. She bit her lip, her body tautening instinctively at his touch.

He looked up at her, his mouth slanting sardonically. 'If it's only a graze, *thespinis*, you're not being very brave about it.'

She said between her teeth, 'Maybe I'd prefer to wait for the doctor.'

He shrugged. 'The Hippocratic oath is not needed for simple first aid,' he returned. 'I am not enjoying this either, Kyria Dryden.'

The oath, she thought, that the medical profession still used. 'I swear by Apollo...' And Apollo himself was here, or so it seemed, kneeling at her feet.

He was deft enough, and even quite gentle, she was forced to admit, but some of the dirt was deeply embedded, and there were tears in her eyes before he'd finished, although she kept her teeth firmly fastened in her bottom lip.

But the smarting was only part of it, she realised. The truth was she didn't want to accept this kind of intimate service from him.

When he had cleaned her arm, he hesitated. 'The shirt is already ruined, I think, so...' He put two fingers in the jagged tear at the side, and ripped it completely down to the hem.

Camilla gasped, dragging the torn edges together. 'How dare you...?' Her voice was unsteady. For one brief instant, his fingers had brushed the curve of her bare breast, and his touch had scalded her.

'So modest?' His voice taunted. 'Your fellow-tourists show more on our beaches every day.'

'But I don't,' she said huskily.

The old woman stepped forward, gesturing him imperatively out of the way. With another shrug, he got to his feet, and walked to the window, turning his back while Camilla's scraped ribs were bathed.

'Arianna,' he tossed over his shoulder, 'you will provide Kyria Dryden with a blouse from your wardrobe as a temporary measure.'

'Of course, I shall be pleased. She can come upstairs to my room, and choose. Petros can examine her there too.'

He frowned. 'Is that necessary?'

'But of course.' Arianna Xandreou looked scandalised. 'Such a procedure requires privacy.'

His frown deepened. 'Then stay with her—all the time, you understand?'

He'd spoken in English, so presumably Camilla wasn't to be left in any doubt either.

'What the hell are you implying?' she demanded.

'I intend to ensure you do not turn this accident to your advantage, *thespinis*.'

'What do you think I'm going to do—steal something?' Camilla pulled away from the old woman's restraining hand, her eyes blazing. 'God, you've an almighty nerve.'

'And I think the same of you, *thespinis*. You will play no tricks in this house.'

Her lips were parting to tell him unequivocally what she thought of him, when the door opened and a young man, swarthy and stockily built, wearing glasses, walked in. He paused, surveying the tableau in front of him.

'I understand I have a new patient,' he remarked. 'A road accident, *ne*? Thank you,

Eleni.' The old woman stepped back, and he inspected her handiwork critically, and nodded. 'You are lucky, *thespinis*. I have known similar incidents where skin grafts have been needed. But you, I think, will be left without a scar. A shot, maybe, to protect against infection and you will be as good as new.'

Spiro Xandreou took him to one side, and said something softly in Greek.

'*Po, po, po.*' The doctor's brows lifted sharply. 'Then I should examine without delay. Eleni can act as chaperon.'

'This is ridiculous,' Camilla protested. 'I'm fine.'

The doctor smiled at her. 'I'm sure that is true. You seem a perfectly healthy young woman. But your pregnancy is in its early stages. We need to establish that all is well.'

'Pregnancy?' Camilla stared at him stupidly. 'What are you talking about? I'm not pregnant.'

'So you lied.' Spiro Xandreou's voice was almost gloating. 'I knew it.' He walked to the door of the *saloni*, and threw it wide, his face a mask of icy anger. 'You will leave my house, *thespinis*, and not come back.'

His voice dropped to pure menace. 'And you will never trouble me or mine again. That is, if you know what's good for you. Now go.'

CHAPTER THREE

CAMILLA stared at him.

She said quietly, 'I think you must be insane, Kyrios Xandreou. Or has your womanising now reached such proportions that you can't even tell one girl from another?'

'How dare you speak to me like that?' His voice was molten. 'How dare you...?'

Camilla met his gaze. Eyes dark as obsidian, she thought with a strange clarity, and as hard as flint. But with a small flame burning...

Just as she was burning inside.

'Oh, I dare.' She drew a deep angry breath. 'Because it wasn't me that you—seduced and abandoned in Athens a few months ago. It was my younger sister, Katie.' A sob rose in her throat. 'And you can't even remember what she really looks like—you bastard.'

Her words fell into a silence so profound it was almost tangible.

It was broken by the doctor, his face expressionless. 'I think, my dear Nic, there has been some misunderstanding. Now, if you'll excuse me, I will go up to my other patient.'

As he turned away, Camilla caught his arm. 'Just a moment—please. You called this man— Nic?'

'*Ne, thespinis*. Is something wrong?'

37

She swallowed. 'You mean—he's not—Spiro?'

The doctor looked astonished. 'Spiro is Kyrios Xandreou's younger brother, *thespinis*. He was also injured in an accident, a short while ago, rather more seriously than yourself. In fact, I should be with him now. If you will call at the clinic in town tomorrow morning, I will prescribe some medication for you—as a precaution only, you understand,' he added kindly, misunderstanding the sudden pallor of her face. 'Infection breeds fast in our climate.'

He nodded briskly, and left the room, Arianna sliding after him.

Camilla found herself alone with Nic Xandreou.

She ran the tip of her tongue round her dry lips. 'You thought I was Katie,' she said. 'I thought you were Spiro. We've been at cross purposes from the start.'

'So it would seem.' His voice was even.

'But Katie's only just eighteen,' she protested. 'You must have known I was older than that.'

He shrugged. 'I thought Spiro had been deceived.' His glance flicked over her. 'There was also the initial on your shirt—a C, presumably for Catherine.'

She said quietly, 'My name is Camilla.' She looked down at the tiled floor. 'I've said some pretty harsh things. I'm sorry, but I was just so upset for Katie.'

'You are loyal to your family,' he returned flatly. 'I don't blame you for that. It's a quality I share.'

'Was Spiro badly hurt in the accident?' she asked in a low voice.

He shrugged again. 'He has a broken leg and a bump on the head. Time and rest will cure them both.'

She tried a small smile. 'Well, it could have been very much worse.' She paused. 'That's why he never turned up at the airport. I just wish someone had let us know. Katie will be so relieved when she knows the truth.' She waited, but he said nothing.

She tried again. 'I'll go straight back to the hotel, and explain.'

'Not,' he said, 'like that, I think.'

She realised where his gaze was directed and dragged the torn edges of her top together again, flushing.

'Well, perhaps not.'

He said curtly, 'I will take you to my sister's room. Come.'

Camilla took a step forward and faltered, her legs shaking under her.

He turned at the door, staring back at her. 'What now?' he demanded impatiently.

'Just reaction, I think.' She tried to force a smile. 'If you could—give me a moment.'

He muttered something succinct and angry under his breath, and came striding back. Before she could guess what he intended, he had swung her off her feet into his arms, and was carrying her across the *saloni* and out into a large hall.

'What the hell are you doing?' Camilla gasped furiously. She braced her hands against his chest, but it was like trying to overturn a brick wall. Except no wall had ever been so warm—so smooth—so sensuous to the touch. She could feel, she realised with an unnerving tingle of awareness, his heart beating under her fingers ...

She said breathlessly, 'Put me down at once.'

'Be still,' he snapped back.

He was very strong. She was slim, but no featherweight, yet he went up the wide, shallow sweep of the marble staircase without a pause.

In the gallery above, he shouldered open a door and went in. It was a large, light room, all pale wood and floating pastel drapes. Arianna was not there, and Nic Xandreou clicked his tongue in sharp annoyance before depositing Camilla without particular gentleness on the edge of the wide, soft bed.

She watched him walk to the tall wardrobes which lined one wall, and fling open a door. He took a shirt, classic in heavy white silk, from a hanger and tossed it to her.

'You can use this,' he ordained.

'I think I'll stay as I am,' she returned quickly. The shirt was clearly very expensive, and the thought of having to struggle to remove her ripped top over her sore shoulder and arm didn't appeal at all. There were some pins in her bag, she remembered. She could make herself decent until she had Katie to help her change.

Nic Xandreou frowned slightly. 'You are in pain?' he guessed.

'Stiffening up a little,' she admitted.

Nic extended his arms in front of him. 'Can you still do this?'

'I think so.' Camilla raised her own arms slightly in imitation.

Nic leaned down, and in one swift movement whipped the torn top over her head and off, baring her to the waist.

'Oh.' Camilla snatched up Arianna's shirt, and held it as a shield in front of her naked breasts, as a wave of frantic embarrassed colour engulfed her. 'How—how dare you?'

'There was no question of daring.' He sounded almost bored. 'You needed assistance, and there was no one else.'

'But that doesn't give you the right...'

A faint smile twisted the corners of the firm mouth. He said softly, 'In my house, Kyria Camilla, I assume whatever rights I choose. Now, I will await you downstairs.'

At the door, he paused, looking back at her, the smile deepening with disturbing mockery.

He said, 'I am glad to know you will not be scarred. Your body is very beautiful.'

And he walked out of the room, leaving Camilla, lips parted in shock, staring after him.

It took her a while to recover her composure. She had never been treated like that in her life before—never been made to feel so vul-

nerable—so frighteningly aware of her
womanhood.

Nic Xandreou wasn't just a powerful and attractive man, she decided grimly. He was
dangerous in all kinds of ways she'd never
envisaged.

She might have said some harsh things to
him, but he'd more than redressed the balance
with that parting shot of his, she thought as
she struggled into Arianna's shirt, her fingers
fumbling the silk-covered buttons into their
holes.

From now on she would be ultra-careful in
any dealings she had with him.

There was a tiny tiled shower-room opening
from the bedroom, which also contained a
washbasin. Looking in the mirror, Camilla
realised for the first time that her face was
smeared with dirt from her fall, and her hair
was tangled and dusty, and she found that she
wanted very much to burst into tears.

But that was just foolish weakness, she told
herself as she washed swiftly and dragged a
comb through her hair. For a moment, she was
half tempted to leave it loose on her shoulders.
It framed her face appealingly, making her look
softer—more relaxed, she thought, lifting some
of the heavy chestnut strands in her fingers.

She stopped right there. What on earth was
she thinking of? She wasn't there to relax, or
make any kind of impression—particularly on
someone like Nic Xandreou, she thought with

self-disgust. She pulled her hair back severely, securing it almost savagely with the barrette.

She came out on to the gallery, and stood for a moment, looking around her. There were a number of other doors on both sides of her, all inimically closed, and between them alcoves had been carved into the walls to display special ceramics and other precious objects.

Camilla's eye was caught by one figurine in particular, and she walked down the gallery to take a closer look. It was a bronze, about three feet high, of a young man with a face as proud and beautiful as an eagle's.

The god Apollo, she wondered, or just the owner of the house, and could anyone tell the difference anyway? But it was a powerful and arresting piece, to say the least.

In fact, the whole villa was quite magnificent, she thought, and maybe that was the trouble—because it was more a showplace than a home, expensive but oddly cold and empty.

She heard the sound of an opening door, and turned to see Arianna and the doctor emerging together from one of the rooms. They walked away from her towards the stairs, too absorbed in conversation to notice her, and disappeared downstairs and out of sight.

So that must be Spiro's room, she realised, swallowing. Spiro whom she'd never even seen.

Impulsively, she went to the door, and knocked. There was a pause then a weary voice said, '*Peraste*,' and she went in.

Spiro Xandreou was lying on a couch near tall windows opening on to a balcony. He was a younger, gentler version of his brother, his good looks muted by pain and shock. He was leaning back, his eyes closed, and the snowy cast on his leg, coupled with the greyness beneath his tanned skin, gave him an air of acute vulnerability.

She said quietly, 'Spiro?' and he opened dazed dark eyes and stared at her.

'*Pya iste*?' he demanded.

'I'm Camilla—Katie's sister.' She smiled at him. 'We arrived on Karthos today to look for you.'

He went on staring at her, his brows drawing together. '*Then sas katalaveno,*' he said. 'I do not understand,' he added in English. 'What do you want?'

'I've come here with Katie,' she said. 'She must have mentioned me.'

He shook his head, his anxious look deepening. 'I do not know you. I do not know any Katie.'

Camilla's heart sank. 'Of course you do.' She tried to sound encouraging. 'You met her in Athens at Easter, and you were coming to London to see her. Only you had this accident, so we've come to you instead.'

'What are you saying?' His voice rose. 'Who are you?'

As Camilla hesitated, uncertain how to proceed, the door behind her was flung open, and Nic Xandreou's voice, molten with anger, said, 'This is intolerable, *thespinis*. My brother must have peace. How dare you intrude on him?'

He took her sound arm, and urged her out of the room, not gently.

Camilla tried to hang back as she was hustled towards the stairs.

'I'm sorry if I've trespassed in some way,' she said. 'But it was Spiro, after all, I came here to see in the first place.'

'In my house you see no one without my permission.'

Camilla lifted her chin. 'And, if I'd asked for permission, would it have been given?'

'No,' he said curtly. 'I only hope your intervention has done no actual harm.'

'I fail to see how a few words from me could affect a broken leg,' she said angrily. 'I know you're concerned about him, but I have my sister to think of.' She paused. 'I also thought Spiro might appreciate some news of her.'

'And did he?'

'Well, no.' Camilla found herself being escorted swiftly and inexorably out of the house, with no chance of saying goodbye to Arianna or asking the doctor about Spiro's condition, she realised with vexation. 'He seemed— confused.'

Nic's firm mouth tightened as he assisted her without particular finesse into the passenger seat of a serviceable-looking Jeep waiting at the front entrance. Her bag, she saw, was waiting for her on the seat, depriving her of any excuse to return. He seemed to think of everything.

'Spiro's recovery will not be assisted by any kind of harassment,' Nic Xandreou said as he started the engine.

Camilla sighed. 'I truly didn't intend that. I just wanted to say—hello.'

'Well, now you have done so,' he said dismissively. 'So let that be an end to it.'

But it couldn't be the end, Camilla thought as the Jeep swung down the drive. It was only the beginning . . .

She stiffened as she caught sight of the scooter at the side of the road. 'Oh, what am I going to do about that?'

'You will do nothing,' he said grimly. 'I have examined the machine, and it was not fit to be on the road even before the accident. Where did you get it?'

'From someone called Andonis.' She produced the card from her bag. 'I got this from the hotel.'

He shot it a frowning glance. 'Ah, yes, the Dionysius. Of course.' He hit the steering-wheel with an exasperated fist. 'I should have known. How many times has he been warned in the past?' He shook his head. 'Never again.'

'I'll go along with that. No matter what it costs, I'll rent a car.'

'You intend to remain on Karthos?' He shot her an unsmiling look.

'Of course. Katie will naturally want to spend every moment with Spiro, and I can enjoy a normal holiday.'

He said bleakly, 'I regret that will not be possible.'

'Why—does Karthos only cater for eccentrics?' Camilla tried to make a feeble joke, to dispel the sudden cold feeling inside her.

'It would be better for you to return to your own country, and take your sister with you.'

She said huskily, 'You mean while Spiro recovers. But he isn't that badly hurt, and Katie will want to help look after him.'

'Her services will not be necessary.' He did not look at her. His attention appeared to be concentrated on the corkscrew road they were descending.

'That's not for you to say.' Camilla kept her tone level. 'You seem to have forgotten that she and Spiro are engaged to be married...'

'I have sanctioned no such engagement,' he returned harshly. 'Nor shall I. It is you that has the poor memory, *thespinis*. We have resolved the mistaken identities, perhaps, but nothing else has changed, believe me.'

'What do you mean?'

His fingers beat an irritable tattoo on the wheel. 'I thought I had made it clear. I do not accept that your sister or her unborn child has any claim on my family. A girl who is overgenerous with her favours before marriage must accept the consequences,' he added damningly.

'While the man escapes scot-free?' Camilla drew a deep, angry breath. 'What a wonderful double standard.'

Nic Xandreou hunched a shoulder. 'Spiro is young,' he said flatly. 'I will not allow him to ruin his future for one foolish lapse.'

'And what about Katie's future?'

'Your sister is clearly a clever young woman. She'll make out.'

'But you can't dismiss it like that.' Camilla's heart was hammering sickly and painfully. 'They're in love.'

His mouth twisted cynically. 'The first of many times for them both, I have no doubt.'

For Spiro, perhaps, she thought, hating him—hating all the lordly Xandreou males. But not steadfast Katie. She had chosen her mate and given her heart. A rejection like this could scar her for life.

She drew an unsteady breath. 'Has Spiro himself no say in all this?'

He paused. 'He knows he has been at fault,' he said. 'I am the head of our family, and ultimately he will do as he is told.'

'A life sentence.' Camilla's tone was biting.

Nic Xandreou shrugged again. 'I have my own plans for Spiro,' he retorted. 'They do not include your sister, *thespinis*.'

'An arranged marriage, no doubt.' It was chilling to have her original fears confirmed.

'A marriage, certainly, based on proper foundations, with real values and a shared culture.' His profile looked as if it had been cast in bronze. 'Spiro will be a wealthy man one day. He will not throw himself away on the first pretty face to catch his eye.'

'So, if Katie were rich, it would be a different story,' Camilla said bitterly.

'I did not say so. Spiro's wife should, firstly, be a woman of discretion.'

She bit her lip. 'People in love don't always behave very sensibly. Haven't you ever fallen head over heels for someone, Mr Xandreou? Or are you like that bronze statue at the villa—all surface glamour but no heart?'

'You presume altogether too much, *thespinis*.' His voice was ice. 'And my emotions are not at issue.'

'But they must meet—to talk about the baby. You can't prevent their seeing each other for that,' Camilla said desperately.

'There would be no point.'

'That's just your opinion. Spiro may have other ideas,' she said tautly. 'Katie certainly will.'

'The matter is not open to discussion. You serve no purpose by remaining on Karthos, *thespinis*, neither you nor your sister. Go back where you belong.'

'Not until Katie has seen Spiro,' she flung back at him. 'You have no right to keep them apart in this high-handed way. I can understand now why "tyrant" is a Greek word,' she added angrily.

The first buildings of Karthos town were beginning to line the road.

'We will not discuss my rights, if you please,' Nic Xandreou said coldly, 'or call me names. Spiro has no wish to see your sister. In fact, he doesn't even remember her name, or that she ever existed.'

'I don't believe that.' Her voice shook. 'You're just afraid to let them meet each other again. You don't want to lose your influence over Spiro—or let him lead his own life.'

'They could meet a dozen times, I promise you, and it would make no difference.' Nic Xandreou swung the Jeep into the square and brought it to an abrupt halt outside the hotel.

'Why should I listen to any promise of yours—or anything you say, for that matter?' Camilla found the passenger door being wrenched open, and herself being lifted down to the narrow pavement.

'Because that bump on the head has given Spiro amnesia, *thespinis*.' His hands were hard on her shoulders. The dark eyes glittered down at her. 'He remembers nothing and no one before the accident. Are you satisfied now?'

'Oh, no.' Camilla lifted a distressed hand to her mouth, her hazel eyes enormous suddenly. 'It can't be true.'

'You think I would lie about something so serious?' His voice rasped.

'No.' She shook her head. 'Oh, God, poor boy. What are we going to do?'

'You will do nothing,' he said. 'I shall nurse my brother back to health and strength alone.'

'That's what you think.' Camilla tensed with new purpose. 'I won't allow you to dismiss Katie from his life like this.'

He said, 'You think to dictate to me, *thespinis*? A woman, to impose her will on Nic Xandreou?' He laughed harshly. 'Never.'

His hands tightened, and he jerked her towards him. Camilla's swift yelp of pain as he touched her grazed arm was as suddenly silenced by the forceful pressure of his mouth on hers.

She felt the cruel dazzle of the sun on her face, beating against her closed eyelids, as his kiss deepened, taking control, teasing her lips apart to admit the invasion of his tongue.

Her breasts were crushed achingly against his chest. She recognised the taut muscularity of the body pressed against hers with every fibre of her being—as if she'd always known in some secret recess of her soul exactly what it would be like to be in Nic Xandreou's arms. As if she'd been born for this moment alone...

Then, with the same suddenness, she was free. He was breathing unevenly, the dark gaze that burned into hers as hot and relentless as the Greek sun.

He said harshly, 'Don't cross me again, Camilla Dryden—if you know what is good for you.'

He swung himself lithely back into the Jeep, and drove off, leaving her staring after him, a hand pressed in disbelief to her ravaged mouth.

CHAPTER FOUR

CAMILLA'S legs were shaking under her as she made her way through the restaurant area to the outside staircase.

She'd never been kissed so publicly before. In fact, she hadn't been kissed that much at all, and Nic Xandreou's deliberate ravishment of her mouth had been a profound and shattering experience.

Particularly when conducted under the gaze of the hotel staff and half the population of Karthos, she thought, shame and resentment fuelling her anger. She was all too aware of the grins and nudges between the waiters who were preparing the tables for dinner. She heard someone say, 'Xandreou's woman,' and laugh.

What on earth had possessed him? she raged inwardly as she went upstairs, avoiding a sullen look of disapproval from Kostas's wife Maria, who was hosing down the courtyard.

A gesture of contempt, perhaps, for the sister of a girl who'd allowed herself to be too easily seduced? Well, he'd misjudged both Katie and herself, as he'd find out to his cost, she promised herself wrathfully.

And if he imagined he could humiliate her into running away, he'd think again about that too.

In the meantime, she'd decided it was best for Katie to remain in the dark about what was going on. She would reunite her sister with Spiro somehow, she was determined about that. But it would serve no purpose to worry Katie unnecessarily, for the time being.

When she went to the clinic in the morning, she would ask the doctor about Spiro's amnesia, its treatment and likely duration. At least then she'd know what they were dealing with.

Nic Xandreou's intransigence was another matter altogether. She'd no idea what could cure that, she thought as she went into the bedroom.

The splash of the shower ceased as she entered the room, and Katie emerged from the small bathroom, a towel wrapped sarong-like around her, running her hands through her damp hair. Her eyes widened when she saw her sister.

'Milla—what's happened?'

Which particular incident did she have in mind? Camilla asked herself in silent irony. Aloud she said, 'I did a really stupid thing, love. I hired one of the local scooters, and fell off.'

Katie looked horrified. 'But you could have been killed.'

'Could have been, but wasn't.' Camilla kept her tone light. 'I'm now cured of living dangerously.' Or I hope I am, she added silently. 'What have you been doing?'

'I slept for ages.' Katie began towelling her hair. 'Then I walked down to the beach and had a swim. The water was wonderful. You should have been with me.'

'Yes.' Camilla collected a handful of fresh undies and started for the shower. 'I really wish I had been.'

'The beach was really crowded,' Katie went on. 'I kept thinking how wonderful it would be if I looked up and saw Spiro coming towards me, just like that first time.' Her voice was very tender, and slightly wistful. 'Falling in love with him was so simple—and right. Now, suddenly, it's all difficult and complicated.'

'But not impossible,' Camilla said bracingly. 'And that's a promise. Now, you decide what I'm going to have for my first Greek meal.' She paused. 'Shall we eat here or at one of the tavernas?'

'Here, I guess.' Katie sounded suddenly listless, her shoulders slumped defeatedly. 'It doesn't really matter.'

Camilla felt her hands clench, and wished they were fastened round Nic Xandreou's throat.

She showered swiftly, flinching as the water touched her grazed skin, but glad at the same time to wash away any lingering contact with Nic Xandreou's mouth and hands. Although the actual memory of the kiss might not be so easy to dismiss, she realised unhappily.

She dressed in a simple jade-green dress with a full wrap-around skirt, brushing her hair out on to her shoulders.

Downstairs, Kostas welcomed them exuberantly, and showed them to a table.

'To drink, ladies?' He handed them menus.

'Orange juice for me,' decided Katie, who'd perked up a little, to Camilla's relief. 'And retsina for my sister.'

'Good, good,' he approved. 'And to eat, may I recommend lamb baked in the oven with tomatoes, garlic and fresh herbs?'

Both girls agreed that that sounded wonderful, and he went off, bellowing noisy instructions towards the kitchen.

'What's retsina?' Camilla asked suspiciously, noting Katie's dancing eyes.

'Resinated white wine. Very Greek. Spiro told me it gets its flavour from the casks it's stored in. You'll love it,' Katie promised.

At first, Camilla found the flavour odd, but her palate soon adapted, and by the time a beaming Kostas brought them appetisers of deep-fried *kalamari*, accompanied by *tsatsiki*, a dip made from yoghurt and cucumbers, she was entirely won over.

The lamb, which came with sliced fried potatoes and green beans, was tender, robustly flavoured and delicious, and Camilla noted thankfully that Katie ate every scrap of her generous helping. Both girls declined the sweet pastries offered for dessert, opting simply for coffee served *sketo*, without sugar.

With the coffee came complimentary glasses of a liqueur tasting of tangerines, served by Kostas who informed them that the entertainment was about to begin.

'Tonight, *thespinis*, we have live bouzouki, and also dance.'

'That sounds like fun.' Katie's face had that wistful look again. 'Spiro took me to some wonderful bouzouki clubs in Athens.'

Camilla couldn't judge the standard of performance when the trio of musicians started up, but the music was lively with an infectious rhythm, and she found herself clapping in time with the beat along with everyone else at the surrounding tables.

A beaming Kostas led off the dancing, with some of the waiters, moving in a slow, almost stately sequence, in line, their hands resting on each other's shoulders.

'That's the *syrto*,' Katie told her. 'It's incredibly old and there are only about six basic steps, but the leader always supplies his own variations.'

Like many burly men, Kostas was agile, and light on his feet, as he dipped and swayed to the music, sinking down to one knee before leaping upright again.

Camilla noticed Maria watching from the hotel doorway, her face sullen and unsmiling. Her whole attitude was in total contrast to her husband's geniality. If theirs had been an arranged marriage, Kostas seemed to have the

worst of the bargain, Camilla thought with
faint amusement.

The beat of the music had changed, and
more people were joining in the dancing,
moving and turning in a chain which wound
between the tables.

Camilla shook her head regretfully when
Kostas beckoned. Her bruised side was aching
too much for that kind of exertion, but Katie
jumped up eagerly.

'Do you think you should?' Camilla put out
a detaining hand.

'Just this once.' There were dreams in Katie's
eyes. 'It brings back so many memories.'

She was young and healthy, Camilla thought
as she sipped her drink. It was wrong to try
and wrap her in cotton wool. And she needed
all the cheering up she could get.

Everyone in the restaurant was watching the
dancing, absorbed in the colour and
movement, but Camilla was suddenly aware,
with a little shiver of unease, that someone was
watching her instead.

The music seemed to fade to a distance, and
the dancers became a blur. She put the tiny
glass down carefully, because her hand was
shaking, and sent a studiedly casual glance
towards the restaurant's trellised entrance.

Nic Xandreou was standing there, hands on
hips. He looked taller than ever in pale grey
trousers, and a shirt in the same colour with a
soft, silky sheen. Across the space that divided
them, his dark eyes met hers in a direct chal-

lenge she felt down to her bones, then switched quite deliberately to where Katie was dancing, her face shining with animation.

Camilla saw his brows lift, and the faint contemptuous smile which twisted his mouth, as he registered the scene before him. He glanced back towards her table. Is this the innocent child, pregnant and broken-hearted? his cynically accusing gaze demanded, louder than any words.

Then he turned, and vanished back into the dark street as silently as he'd come.

Camilla found her heart was hammering, and her mouth suddenly dry. What was he doing there? she asked herself. If he'd come to see Katie, he couldn't have chosen a worse moment. He'd be convinced now that she was just another silly, pretty English girl hell-bent on a good time. She could have screamed with vexation.

The music ended, and Katie returned, glowing.

'That was wonderful,' she said. 'Spiro would be proud of me.' She gave her sister a swift hug. 'Everything's going to be all right. I know it is.'

Camilla returned her smile, but with constraint. With a sinking heart, she thought, I wish I could be so sure.

The next morning found her climbing the steep cobbled street that led up through the centre of town to the clinic.

To her relief, Katie had not pressed her initial offer to accompany her, agreeing to see her later on the beach.

Quite apart from her various aches and pains, Camilla had found sleep elusive the previous night. She had lain listening to Katie's gentle breathing, trying to make plans—to decide principally what to do if the doctor refused to help them.

It was a possibility she couldn't discount. He was clearly a friend of the Xandreou family, and might well agree with Nic Xandreou that Katie was a minor indiscretion, easily brushed aside.

She sighed as she traversed the crowded pavements, where shop displays overflowed into the open air. She found herself edging round stands of beautifully tooled leather bags, woven rugs in traditional patterns and cascades of embroidered linens and wall-hangings. At any other time, she would have lingered for a closer look at the goods on offer, but she had the uneasy feeling that there wasn't a second to be lost.

Nic Xandreou was a powerful man, with the island in his pocket. And she and Katie were outsiders, totally isolated. She couldn't forget that for a minute.

Nor could she forget the scorch of his kiss on her mouth—nor, more fundamentally, his parting warning. For her own peace of mind, she should keep out of Nic Xandreou's way,

and common sense suggested a strategic retreat
back to England.

But, in spite of her personal misgivings, it
was Katie's interests she had to consider, and
those of her unborn child. Katie had come to
Karthos to be reunited with the man she loved.

And I've promised to help, she thought. I
can't go back on that now simply because Nic
Xandreou alarms and disturbs me.

The clinic was housed in an old building, its
bell-tower revealing it as a former monastery.
But once inside the rather forbidding entrance
Camilla found the facilities were a dream of
ultra-modernity. Petros, in an immaculate
white coat, was standing talking to the recep-
tionist, and he came across to Camilla at once.

'How are you today, *thespinis*?' His smile
was friendly. 'No ill effects from your fall—no
raised temperature, or headaches?'

'I'm a bit stiff and sore, but otherwise fine.
I really don't need any antibiotics.' She paused.
'But I would like to consult you about some-
thing else.'

'Of course.' He opened a door, and waved
her ahead of him. Camilla walked in, and
paused, half dazzled by the blast of strong sunlight which greeted her, turning the rest of the
large room to shadow. The room was domi-
nated, she saw, by a huge desk, and, straight
ahead of her, long windows stood open, giving
access to a walled garden with a colonnaded
walkway, presumably once used by the monks.

'My office,' Petros told her as he closed the door. 'For my sins I am also the clinic director.'

'You've certainly chosen the loveliest room.' Camilla looked with open delight at the central square of grass, where a small fountain danced from the cupped hands of a discreetly veiled stone nymph, while surrounding the fountain were roses, great, shaggy, untamed masses of them in every shade from crimson and deep copper to the palest cream.

'Sit down, *thespinis*. How may I help you?'

Camilla took a deep breath. 'I want to ask you about Spiro Xandreou's amnesia,' she said. 'I suppose you know why my sister and I are on Karthos?'

'The matter has been mentioned.' The doctor's face was discreetly enigmatic.

'Then we're very much at your mercy. Please—how long will it be before Spiro remembers things again?'

He shook his head. 'You ask me something I cannot answer. Sometimes the condition changes slowly. In other cases, a jog to the memory can restore it suddenly and completely.' He sighed. 'But Spiro fights his condition. It frightens him to realise that much of his past has become a blank, and this increases his confusion.'

Camilla grimaced. 'Then my visit yesterday really didn't help. I wish I'd been told what was wrong.'

'The family does not wish his condition generally known. This is a small island with simple people. A broken leg is understood, something in the mind less so.'

Camilla nodded. 'You mentioned a jog to his memory. Do you think, maybe, seeing my sister again could be just the jolt he needs?'

Petros's face sobered. 'It is certainly possible,' he said, after a pause.

'Then can you arrange it?'

He spread his hands in apology. 'I regret it is not permitted. Nic—Kyrios Xandreou—has given orders that neither you nor your sister is to be admitted to the villa, or allowed to see Spiro. I'm sorry.'

'Oh, God.' Camilla, speaking through gritted teeth, hardly recognised her own voice. 'The bastard.'

She remembered the searing pressure of his mouth on hers and thought, Judas.

Petros looked shocked. 'You must not say such a thing, *thespinis*. You do not understand. Since Nic was quite young, he has had to be the patriarch to his family, and it has not been easy. He seeks only to protect them.' He paused, looking uncomfortable. 'Perhaps to keep them from mistakes that he knows will only lead to great unhappiness.'

'I'm sure the mighty Mr Xandreou has never put a foot wrong in his life,' Camilla said bitterly. 'He's the golden boy through and through.'

The doctor shook his head. 'Not always, *thespinis*,' he corrected gently. 'The loss of his parents—then his marriage, and the death of his wife—all these were tragedies for him. And they have left their mark, I think.'

Camilla gasped. 'He's a widower?' she asked huskily. It was the last thing she'd expected to hear. She bit her lip, remembering how she'd accused him of being without a heart—without feeling. Clearly that had not been true—once. But surely it should make him more understanding of Katie and Spiro...

She said, 'Couldn't you talk to him—from a medical point of view? Convince him that letting Katie see Spiro would be worth trying at least?'

'I can try,' he said. 'But I guarantee nothing. Nic is my friend—and a friend to everyone on Karthos.' He gestured around him wryly. 'He provided this clinic at his own expense. But, like his father and grandfather before him, he is an autocrat. His word has always been law, and he expects no argument with his decisions.'

Camilla got to her feet. 'Then perhaps it's time there was,' she returned crisply.

His brows rose. 'You are a brave woman, *thespinis.*' The internal telephone rang on his desk, and he lifted the receiver. As he listened, Camilla saw him begin to frown. He said something quietly in his own language, and rang off.

He said, 'There is something I must see to, *thespinis*, if you'll excuse me.' He paused, looking faintly embarrassed. 'I hope I may offer you some coffee before you go?'

'There's no need.' Camilla hesitated, glancing at her watch.

'No, it is my pleasure. One moment only, please.'

The door closed behind him.

Camilla walked over to the window, and looked out. The sun-warmed scent of the roses, carried on the faint breeze, seemed to fill the room. Their fragrance and colour caught at her throat—lifted her heart.

She thought, I was right to come here. He's made no promises, but at least he's held out a glimmer of hope.

She heard the door behind her open again.

She said, 'I can't tell you how grateful I am. I'm sure, between us, we can persuade Mr Xandreou to change his mind.'

'Such certainty, *thespinis*.' The silken mockery of an all too familiar voice assailed her ears. 'Now I wouldn't count on a thing.'

For a moment, Camilla stood, frozen to the spot, then slowly she turned and looked across the shadows of the room to the tall man who stood by the doorway. Blocking, she realised, her means of retreat.

'*Kalimera*,' said Nic Xandreou, and smiled at her.

CHAPTER FIVE

CAMILLA said, 'What are you doing here?'

'I knew you were due to see Petros Deroulades here this morning.' The dark gaze went over her coolly, absorbing the pale blue button-through dress, as if its chain-store origins were quite apparent to him. 'I thought perhaps we should talk—on neutral territory.'

'And he just went along with it,' she said bitterly.

'You must not blame poor Petros,' he said. 'I have—a certain influence here.'

'So he told me.' Camilla drew a breath. 'You're quite the philanthropist, Mr Xandreou. Someone should have told you that charity begins at home.'

'Which is exactly what I wish to discuss.' He moved to the desk and sat on the corner of it, lithe and relaxed. 'Won't you sit down again?'

'I'll stay where I am,' she said curtly. 'Are you telling me you're prepared to lift your embargo on Katie's visiting Spiro?'

'No,' he said. 'I'm sure you know better than that.'

'Then there's no more to be said.' She walked past him to the door, head held high, and twisted the heavy carved handle with mounting frustration.

He said, 'Save your energy, *thespinis*. There is a security device in operation.'

So, for the moment she was trapped. The realisation dried her mouth. She looked at him lounging there, totally the master of the situation, and anger shook her voice.

'Will you let me out of here?'

'When you have heard what I have to say.'

'I'm not interested,' Camilla said huskily. 'Until your attitude changes over Katie, there is nothing to discuss.'

'We will see.' The dark eyes were hooded, enigmatic. 'Where is your sister?'

'At the hotel.' Camilla looked at her watch again. 'And she'll be wondering where I am.'

His mouth twisted. 'I am sure she will have found entertainment.'

'What do you mean by that?'

'As you know, I saw her dancing last night.' His smile was edged. 'She seems to have an affinity with my countrymen. An uninhibited performance.'

'Then your brother must be a good teacher,' she returned, refusing to take the obvious bait. 'He showed her all the steps in person.' One mark to our side, she told herself silently as she saw his lips tighten.

She hurried into speech. 'As a matter of interest, why was he working in that restaurant? It seems an odd way for a future millionaire to earn a crust.'

'You think a man should take his inheritance without effort—without responsibility?' His voice was suddenly harsh. 'That he should enjoy the fruits, and remain in ignorance of how the harvest has been grown?' He shook his head. 'No, Spiro will work, as I have done, in every branch of our business undertakings, and at every level, from the lowliest menial job to top administration.' He paused. 'Good management comes from knowledge and understanding.'

'Of which you have so much, of course.' It nettled her that what he was saying made so much sense; that he was determined not to let Spiro degenerate into just another member of the idle rich. 'So Athens was just part of the menial phase.'

'Yes, but don't pity him too much. There are worse jobs, I promise you,' he added sardonically.

She could believe it, although for the life of her she couldn't imagine Nic Xandreou himself, in spite of his claims, waiting on tables, or emptying garbage. Someone would have been around to flatten his path, and make sure he didn't roughen his hands too much on his way to the boardroom.

She found herself suddenly remembering those hands as they'd touched her. Powerful, she thought, and strong as steel, but the long fingers strangely sensitive.

Her own were small and workmanlike, as they'd had to be. She found she was spreading them against the door behind her, as if seeking reassurance from its solidity and weight.

She said, 'And your sister Arianna—will she take her turn as a chambermaid?'

'No. For a woman, it is different.'

She thought, Not where I come from.

Aloud, she said, 'And I suppose you have a nice dynastic marriage worked out for her too.' She shook her head. 'Don't you ever get tired of dominating people—controlling their lives?'

He said tautly, 'I care for my family, *thespinis*. I am responsible for them, and for all those who depend on me. I cannot afford to become weary or indifferent to these responsibilities.'

'And Arianna's just content to—go with the flow.' Camilla found it hard to believe. She remembered the petulance in the dark eyes, the sullen curve to the girl's mouth.

'She knows where her duty lies,' he returned flatly. 'And so does Spiro. So, do not hope, or allow your sister to do so. She has no place in his life.'

'And if Arianna were in the same situation as Katie, Mr Xandreou—what then?' she demanded.

She looked at him, and he was darkness against the brilliance of the sun.

He said softly, 'I would find the man, and kill him with my own hands.'

The words died away, but their menace remained almost tangibly. It was suddenly difficult to breathe. She needed air, and she ran, almost stumbling in her haste to the open glass doors and the escape they seemed to offer.

But even that was an illusion. The garden was totally enclosed in its high walls.

The heat beat down on her like a clenched fist. The scent of roses was almost overpowering, and the air was heavy with the hum of working bees, and the ceaseless rasp of unseen cicadas. She walked to the fountain, and let the cool water play on her wrists, as she strove to calm her errant pulses.

This might have been a monastery once, she thought, her heart hammering unsteadily, but there'd been something altogether older and more primitive than Christianity in that room just then. And it was around her now, in this blazing sun, and bleached walls, reminding her that Greece was a country where once pagan gods had ruled with their own savage codes of blood and vengeance.

She'd come to Karthos as a latter-day avenging Fury, but now the tables were turned, and in some strange way she was the quarry, not the pursuer.

In one shady corner, she saw the spreading branches and glossy leaves of a laurel. Apollo's tree, she thought. Sacred to him because it was supposed to hold the spirit of a girl he'd loved—the river nymph Daphne who'd run from him, and turned herself to wood to escape capture.

Had she hated him or simply been afraid of the power he exerted? Either way, Camilla could understand that kind of desperation. Because her own dark Apollo had followed her now, and was standing watching her, hands on hips. He was more formally dressed than she had ever seen him, but he'd discarded the jacket of his light suit, and the sleeves of his white shirt had been turned back to reveal his tanned forearms. His tie, too, had been loosened, as if he'd grown impatient with its constriction. As if the normal trappings of civilisation were only a veneer, easily discarded. As well they might be . . .

His gaze was almost meditative, lingering on the loose waves of her chestnut hair, the quiver of her parted lips, and the thrust of her rounded breasts against the thin material of her dress. She was covered from throat to knee, but she might as well have been naked, she realised dazedly.

She'd never been so physically aware of any man in her life before, or so helpless in controlling her own reactions. She was actually beginning to shake under the dark intensity of his eyes.

The silence between them was charged— dangerous.

She took a step back, and found herself caught fast, anchored to the spot by the trailing briar of a bush of deep crimson roses.

'Oh, no.' She twisted, struggling to free herself, shying away with a yelp as Nic walked across to her. 'I can manage.' Her voice sounded oddly breathless.

'Keep still, and don't be a fool,' he cautioned sharply. 'I don't need another torn garment of yours laid to my account.' With infinite care, he detached her skirt from the clinging tendrils. 'Nor any further marks on your skin,' he added quietly.

'Thank you.' Camilla swallowed, smoothing the snagged fabric over her thighs.

'*Parakalo.*' There was a note of veiled amusement in his voice. He leaned past her, deftly picking a rose, a folded bud of dark velvet, from the offending bush.

'So soft, *ne*?' His voice was almost teasing. 'So beautiful.' He brushed the dusky petals against her cheek. 'So exquisitely scented.' The rose touched the corner of her startled mouth, forcing a gasp from her. 'But beware,' he added silkily. 'Like a woman, this beauty hides sharp thorns.'

He was altogether too close to her. She could almost feel the warmth of his body, as if he were touching her in earnest, drawing her against him, holding her near.

Instead of just—stroking her with that damned flower. He was brushing it against the pulse in her throat now, and down to the demure rounded neckline of her dress. And down further to the first soft swell of her breasts...

She could feel herself shivering suddenly, her nipples hardening in anticipation against the thin, revealing fabric.

Oh, God, she thought. What am I doing? What's happening to me?

He was playing some kind of game with her, and she knew it, even if she didn't fully understand what it was. She was supposed to be the cool one, the girl who was practical and in charge, and she couldn't allow him to destroy her equilibrium like this.

Because, like him, she was the head of her family, and she had to face him, challenge him on equal terms.

She stepped away, deliberately out of range. 'Did you arrange this interview just to discuss horticulture?'

'Is that what we were doing? It was not my purpose—however enjoyable.' He paused, the dark eyes glinting, letting her know he'd been well aware of her body's involuntary reaction to his teasing. He was still holding the rose, turning it slowly in his fingers. He said, 'I have a business proposition to put to you.'

'Oh.' Camilla stiffened. 'What kind of proposition?'

'A financial deal. I realise on reflection that I was over-ready to dismiss your claims. But your appearance at my home took me by surprise, you understand.'

'You thought Katie would just let Spiro vanish from her life?' she asked incredulously. 'That she'd make no effort to find him?'

He shrugged. 'She would not be the first to find that a holiday amour can have—repercussions. She might have decided to cut her losses—put it down to experience.'

'But it wasn't like that,' she said desperately. She beat her clenched fist into the palm of her other hand. 'I wish Katie were here to convince you.'

'It would prove nothing.' He paused again. 'Would she have been so anxious to trace my brother, I wonder, if he'd been simply a waiter in a restaurant? If he hadn't told her that he was a Xandreou?'

'She didn't believe his claims,' she said wearily.

'And now?'

'Nothing has changed.' Camilla hesitated. 'I've mentioned nothing about you, Spiro, the villa—any of it.'

'Why not?'

'To protect her from the hurt of knowing she's not considered good enough for your family.'

His mouth tightened. 'Do you have no man to speak for you?' he asked. 'No father—no brothers?'

'We're alone.'

'Then any negotiation must be with you.' He paused. 'I am prepared on certain conditions to settle a sum of money on your sister, which, suitably invested, will provide support for her child.'

Camilla tensed. 'Conditions?' she repeated. 'What conditions?'

'They are simple,' he said. 'She will receive the money through an agreement drawn up by our respective lawyers only if she promises to leave Karthos immediately, and makes no attempt to contact Spiro in the future.'

She couldn't believe what she was hearing. Nic Xandreou was proposing to write Katie out of Spiro's life, as if she were some unimportant tax loss.

She said, 'And if Spiro himself tries to contact her—when he recovers?'

'He will not.'

A few brief words, she thought shakily, to pass sentence of death on a love-affair.

She said, too evenly, 'As simple as that.'

'That's how it has to be,' he said. 'Or no deal. I want the matter over, before more harm is done. And be thankful I offer this much,' he added icily. 'I saw her last night at the Dionysius. If she behaved with equal freedom in Athens, Spiro may not be the only candidate for the fatherhood of her baby.'

Camilla's face flamed. 'How dare you say such a thing?'

'Because it's true,' he flung back at her. 'She is no saint. Like all the rest, she comes to Greece looking for romance—a little adventure with a man. And you, Camilla, you are no different either.'

He tossed the rose away from him suddenly, as if it had burned his hand. 'Let us speak the truth to each other—the truth our bodies have already uttered. If I wanted you, I could take you, and we both know it.'

His words fell into a hot and stinging silence.

The blood was pounding in Camilla's head. She drew back her arm, and slapped him hard across the face. His head fell back in shock, and he swore briefly and violently in Greek, as his hand went up to touch his bruised cheekbones.

She saw anger and disbelief flare in his eyes, then he reached for her, and she dodged past him, and ran for the open glass doors.

Although there was no sanctuary there in the locked and shadowed room, she thought, her heart pounding as she realised he was coming after her. No friendly laurel tree either to transform and protect her from his pursuit.

But, like a small miracle, the office door was standing open. And there were people there— Petros Deroulades, and beside him Arianna Xandreou, their faces pictures of sheer astonishment.

Camilla said breathlessly, '*Kalimera*,' and kept running.

Her legs were still shaking under her when she arrived back at the hotel. Fortunately she'd managed to hail a cruising taxi just outside the clinic, and she huddled in its back seat, resisting the impulse to peer over her shoulder to see if Nic Xandreou was still chasing her.

She found herself wondering, absurdly, what would have happened if the original nymph had stood her ground and cracked Apollo as hard as she could. Maybe he'd have abandoned his seduction, and she could have gone on happily swimming in her river.

And maybe not. It was never a good thing to cross the ancient gods. Or Nic Xandreou, for that matter, although his slap across the face had been fully deserved.

Presumably he was so used to women going down like ninepins under the force of his sexual charisma that he'd taken her compliance for granted.

Well, he could nurse the realisation that he was wrong about her along with his bruised face.

He was wrong, too, if he thought that Katie could simply be bought off.

There isn't enough money in the world, Mr Xandreou, she thought savagely as she paid off the taxi driver.

Maria was at Reception when she called for the room key. The older woman gave her a venomous look, then disappeared behind the beaded curtain behind the desk which led to the family quarters. A moment later, Kostas appeared, wiping his moustache. His normal dazzling smile had disappeared, and his expression seemed stuck at some halfway mark between wariness and embarrassment.

'Kyria Dryden.' He weighed the key in his hand. 'I regret there is a problem. A mistake in reservations. Your room is needed for other people—a prior booking, you understand. I must ask you to vacate it tomorrow.'

Camilla felt as if she'd been poleaxed.

'But you can't do that. We have a fortnight's booking, paid in advance,' she protested.

He spread his hands in a sketch of an apology. 'All your money will be refunded. I am sorry for the inconvenience.'

'Inconvenience, you call it.' Camilla's voice shook. She was angrily aware that Maria was watching with sour triumph from behind the curtain. 'If you've made a mistake, the least you can do is find us another room.'

Kostas looked uneasier than ever. 'That would be difficult for me, *thespinis*. I don't want trouble. It would be better if you left Karthos, I think. Take the ferry—go to Zakynthos. I have a friend with a hotel in Alikes—very pretty, very quiet.'

'Oh, I see.' Camilla was getting more furious by the second. 'You don't just want us out of the hotel but off the island too. Tell me, Kostas, would Mr Nic Xandreou have any hand in this?'

A dull flush showed under his skin. '*Thespinis*, this is not easy for me, but it is impossible you stay in my hotel. I give you back your money, and you go, *ne*?'

Camilla picked up her key with all the dignity she could assume. She said, 'Don't worry. We wouldn't dream of staying on.'

She was near to tears as she went upstairs. She hadn't escaped from Nic Xandreou at all, nor scored even a moral victory. That had been illusion. Even at a distance he had the power to harm her.

One phone call from the clinic was all it had taken. An act of spiteful retaliation for that slap on the face. And Kostas, like a good vassal, was carrying out the orders from his overlord.

I should have kept my temper, she berated herself as she unfastened the shutters and stepped out on to the balcony. Let him think I was prepared to negotiate. Bought us some more time here. Now I've blown it completely.

We'll have to go back to England, she thought, and get the best legal advice we can afford. Which means that Katie's love-affair is going to be distorted into a sordid wrangle over child support. And Spiro, in his blank, confused world, won't even know.

And now she would have to find Katie and break the bad news to her—all of it.

She was turning away, when she saw a familiar figure walk into the restaurant area below, and stand looking round her, hand on hip, head arrogantly high.

Arianna Xandreou, she thought. Sent by big brother to check we've got our marching orders. She picked up the silk blouse she'd laundered the night before, and left the bedroom.

On the stairs, she met Arianna on her way up. The Greek girl treated her to a mischievous smile.

'So,' she said. 'You called up the storm and survived. I am all admiration.'

'Oh.' Camilla paused, taken aback. 'You—you know what happened?'

'Not everything, and I did not dare ask. I don't have your courage, *po*, *po*, *po*. My brother is not accustomed to opposition.'

'Then he'll have to get used to it.' Camilla drew a furious breath. 'Because I'll go on fighting him every step of the way—even if he does get me deported from Karthos. And you can tell him so.'

Arianna shrugged a slim shoulder. 'I don't think so,' she said drily. 'But what is this "deport"? You are leaving Karthos?'

'Not of my own free will.' Camilla bit her lip. 'Your brother tried to buy us off, and when I—refused he instructed the hotel to throw us out. We're homeless as from tomorrow.'

Arianna's brows snapped together. She said flatly, 'No, Nic would not do such a thing. He would despise it. It is the action of a man with a small mind, and though he has many faults he is not that.'

'But Kostas didn't deny it when I asked if your brother was involved,' Camilla argued. 'And I did make him very angry.'

'Yes.' Arianna's tone gloated. 'More angry than I can remember. With Spiro there are often explosions. But Nic—always he stays as cold as ice. So it is good for him that someone does not do as he wants—and even better when that someone is a woman.' She nodded. 'Come, we will talk together.'

Camilla hung back. 'I don't want you to get into trouble with your—family.'

Arianna's smile was impish. 'No problem. And you need me, Camilla Dryden, if your sister is to see Spiro—and make him remember.'

Astounded, Camilla found herself seated at a table, sipping iced peach juice, fresh and tangy in tall glasses.

She said in a low voice, 'You mean you're prepared to help? But why?'

Arianna shrugged. 'Spiro is my brother, and I love him. I want him to be happy, but in his own way, not that of Nic,' she added emphatically. 'And maybe, one day, you can also help me, *ne*?'

'If I can, perhaps,' Camilla agreed warily. The lovely Arianna was clearly up to something, but she couldn't figure out what it was.

'So Nic offered you money.'

'Yes.' Camilla flushed stormily at the memory.

'Do not blame him too much,' Arianna said calmly. 'Life, I think, has taught him that everything and everyone has a price. But you refused him?'

Camilla drank some peach juice. 'Not in so many words,' she said guardedly. 'I just—lost my temper.'

'That is good.' Arianna gave a vigorous nod. 'Because that gives you an excuse to stay—to have more discussions with Nic.'

'I don't think so.' Camilla paused. 'Your brother won't want to see me again.'

Arianna smiled. 'No?' She glanced past Camilla. 'See for yourself.'

Camilla twisted round in her chair in time to see Nic Xandreou, with a face like thunder, stride under the vine-clad archway, and head straight for their table.

The storm she'd summoned up was about to break.

CHAPTER SIX

CAMILLA pushed her chair back and got to her feet, aware that she was trembling.

'Come to evict us in person, Mr Xandreou?' she challenged as he reached them.

Nic Xandreou frowned, his dark gaze stormy as it flicked over her. 'No, *thespinis*, to find my sister.' He looked down at Arianna who was toying with the straw in her glass. 'I saw your car in the square,' he said flatly. 'What are you doing here?'

Arianna shrugged. 'I decided to save Kyria Dryden the trouble of returning the shirt you lent her.' She held up the garment in question. 'Remember?'

'Yes,' he acknowledged after a brief pause. 'I remember.'

It occurred to Camilla exactly what he was recalling to mind, and sudden warmth invaded her face.

'And now we are having a farewell drink together,' the Greek girl added pointedly.

Nic Xandreou turned back to Camilla. 'You are truly leaving?'

He had the unmitigated gall to sound surprised. Camilla's gaze dwelt vengefully on the reddened mark on his cheek. Her only regret was that she hadn't given him a black eye.

She said, clearly and coldly, 'You should know, *kyrie*. You arranged it, after all.'

'I?' His frown deepened. 'Naturally I welcome the wisdom of your decision, but what has it to do with me?'

'Because of you, Camilla and her sister have been told to leave the hotel,' Arianna supplied.

'Nonsense.' He gave Camilla an ironic look. 'You credit me with more influence than I possess, *thespinis*.'

'Naturally you'd deny it,' she returned tautly.

'I am not in the habit of lying.' His mouth tightened. 'Nor have I reason to do so. However I will speak to Kostas Philippides so you may judge for yourself.'

Kostas arrived, his face sullen. Camilla could understand little of the conversation which followed, but the hotel-keeper was clearly on the defensive, hands waving as he gesticulated angrily towards the hotel.

Nic dismissed him with obvious impatience, and gave Camilla a grim look. 'It is Maria, his wife, who demands your departure, *thespinis*. Because of you, a member of her family has been insulted, and she refuses, in consequence, to allow you to stay.'

'Because of me?' Camilla sank back into her chair. 'But that's ridiculous. I've done nothing.'

'You hired a scooter,' Nic reminded her. He sighed angrily. 'I spoke to Andonis about it— warned him he would be reported to the police if he continued to rent out machines in that condition.' His mouth twisted. 'It was not a friendly interview.'

'Andonis is related to Maria?' Camilla asked blankly.

'Her nephew.' He paused. 'Another works here as a waiter.'

'Yes,' she said. He told me how to find you, she thought. And he was the one who called 'Xandreou's woman' after me yesterday.

'Andonis has complained to his aunt. She witnessed your return to the hotel yesterday, it seems, and has told Kostas you are a trouble-maker and also morally suspect.'

'But that's absurd.' Camilla pressed her hands to her hot face as the memory of that parting insult of a kiss tormented her once more. 'She wouldn't turn us out—just for that, surely?'

Nic shrugged. 'She has lived all her life on Karthos,' he said flatly. 'It does little to broaden the mind, believe me. But the root cause of her anger is my threat to Andonis. I have assured Kostas you are blameless, but Maria has a bad temper and a wicked tongue, and his life will be a misery to him unless he carries out her wishes.'

'So, in fact it is true. Camilla and her sister are being turned out of the hotel because of you!' Arianna exclaimed, her eyes glinting.

'I suppose—yes.' He gestured angrily. 'But I could not know that my words with Andonis would have such a repercussion.'

Arianna leaned back in her chair. 'Then we must make amends, Nic.'

'What do you mean?' His tone was biting.

She looked back at him blandly. 'We cannot let two girls, one of them pregnant, be turned on to the streets. We are responsible, my brother, so we must help.' She paused. 'They must stay with us at the Villa Apollo.'

Camilla heard Nic's sharp intake of breath, and froze in shock.

'No,' they both said, in sharp and explosive union.

Arianna laughed. 'So, you agree on something, if only to disagree.' She lifted a graceful shoulder. 'But I think there is no choice.' She paused. 'If not the villa, then the sea house. It is never used, and Soula can look after them.'

'There's no need,' Camilla protested into a loaded silence. 'All we need is another hotel room somewhere . . .'

'That is not so easy.' Arianna pulled a face. 'Karthos is full at this season. And, besides, what has happened to you is an outrage against *philoxenia*—the welcome we Greeks give to the strangers among us.' She turned to Nic. 'Tell her, brother.'

He looked as if he'd been carved from stone. 'Arianna is right,' he said icily. 'You have been wronged because of me, and I must make reparation. I offer you our—hospitality for the remainder of your stay.'

She said between her teeth, 'I'd rather sleep on the beach.'

'But that would not be good for your sister,' Arianna pointed out. 'Also the tourist police do not allow. Better you come to us.'

There was a silence. Nic's face was expressionless, but Camilla had the sensation of harsh emotion barely under control.

At last, he said tautly, 'The sea house is at your disposal, *thespinis*. You will be transferred there tomorrow.' He paused. 'It is at a distance from the Villa Apollo, so we shall be able to respect each other's privacy.'

The warning was unequivocal, Camilla realised. The villa and Spiro were still strictly out of bounds.

'I understand.' She lifted her chin.

'I thought you would.' Nic nodded curtly. 'Now I shall go and make the necessary arrangements.' He looked at his sister. 'And you, Arianna?'

'I have still some shopping.' Her face was guileless.

'Then I'll see you later.' His tone was clipped as his glance flicked once more to Camilla. 'Until tomorrow, *thespinis*.'

Camilla watched his tall figure stride away, and collapsed back in her chair. She said wanly, 'Arianna, you've put me in an impossible position. I—we can't accept this offer.'

'You wish to stay on Karthos, *ne*?' Arianna's smile was cat-like. 'Then that is the important thing—not your pride, or even this quarrel with Nic, which made him hold his hand to his face when he followed you from the garden today,' she added slyly.

Camilla bit her lip. 'Your brother and I are better apart, believe me,' she said constrictedly.

'So, the sea house will be perfect,' Arianna said with a shrug. 'Because Nic never goes there. It was where he spent his honeymoon, so it has bad memories for him.'

'Oh, God,' Camilla said huskily. 'This gets worse all the time. Katie and I are the least people he'd want in a place with such—personal associations.'

'All the more reason for him to keep away,' Arianna returned caustically. 'And Soula will be happy to have someone to look after again. She was our nurse when we were children, and has been with us in America and Australia, so she speaks English.' She leaned forward, eyes gleaming. 'And once you are living in the sea house it can be arranged for your sister and Spiro to see each other again. No problem.' She pushed back her chair. 'Now it would be good if Katie and I met, *ne*?'

Camilla said mechanically, 'Yes, of course. We'll go and find her.'

Her legs were shaking as she got to her feet. The full implications of what she'd agreed to were just starting to sink in. She was about to become the guest of Nic Xandreou, resident on his property, if not actually under his roof.

'No problem'. The phrase—the Greek panacea for everything—echoed mockingly in her mind.

Camilla shivered inwardly. My God, she thought, if only it were true.

They found Katie on the beach. She listened in grave silence while Camilla, with certain prudent exceptions, recounted everything that had happened since their arrival on Karthos.

Katie went very white when she heard the details of Spiro's accident, and its effects, but seemed to accept Arianna's assurance that he was expected to recover fully in time.

'But I should be with him,' she said anxiously. 'He needs me.'

'Of course.' Arianna patted her arm. 'Unfortunately, little one, we now have to persuade my stubborn older brother too.'

Katie gave her a wavering smile. The two girls had taken to each other on sight, rather to Camilla's surprise. Arianna was light years ahead of Katie in sophistication, and, Camilla suspected, guile. They shouldn't have had a thought in common. However...

'A young sister,' Arianna had laughed. 'Just what I always wanted. Spiro told me I would love you.'

'He spoke about me?' Katie asked wistfully.

'Of course. He knew I would be happy for him.' Arianna sighed. 'But Nic was a different story.' She shook her head. 'My God, what a quarrel. The whole of Karthos must have heard it.'

Katie looked troubled. 'Spiro told me there might be—difficulties.'

'My brothers have always fought,' Arianna said serenely. 'It's nothing. But Nic has strong views on marriage. He says like must marry like, or there can be no happiness. And he'd planned a bride for Spiro,' she added almost casually. 'Already there'd been discussions with the girl's family, so he was not pleased when Spiro said he'd made his own choice.

'After all, it was only what Nic had done himself, as Spiro was quick to remind him.' She pulled a face. 'He was so angry. Even after five years, there is still pain for him when he remembers.'

'Well, that's understandable,' Camilla said constrictedly. Although Nic Xandreou was hardly the pattern of the grieving widower, she thought, wondering what his wife had been like. Some gentle doe-eyed Greek girl, no doubt, who'd treated him like a god.

She said, 'If he wants this marriage so much, why doesn't he marry the girl himself?' and was surprised at the sharpness in her voice.

Arianna shrugged. 'There is a saying, ne, that once burned you fear the fire?' Her smile was worldly. 'Besides, Nic amuses himself very well. There is a girl in Athens, and another, I think, in New York. Why should he choose one dish, when a banquet is waiting?'

Why indeed? Camilla thought hollowly.

She got to her feet. 'I'd better start packing if we're moving tomorrow.'

'Shall I help?' Katie sat up.

'No, stay where you are.' Camilla forced a smile. 'Enjoy the sun.'

'And I will stay too,' Arianna said. 'We will talk, Katie *mou*, become friends as well as sisters. Make Spiro happy.'

Arianna certainly knew the right things to say, Camilla thought as she walked back to the hotel. And she was clearly going to be an important ally in the battle to reunite Spiro and Katie.

So why do I feel there's more going on than meets the eye? she wondered restively. Beware the Greeks when they come bearing gifts. That was the old saying, although it seemed ungrateful to remember it.

The hotel seemed totally deserted as she threaded her way between the tables in the courtyard, but she had the oddest feeling that she was being watched as she went up the outside stairway to the room. She glanced back over her shoulder, but could see no one. Perhaps the malignant Maria's evil eye was operating at a distance, she thought, deriding herself for being over-fanciful.

The room was cool and shady, the shutters closed, and the thin tan-coloured drapes drawn too. Camilla reluctantly lifted the empty cases on to one of the beds. She hadn't bargained for packing up so soon. But then, if she was honest, she hadn't envisaged anything that had befallen her on Karthos so far. Anything — or anyone.

The image of Nic Xandreou rose in her mind so clearly and sharply that he might have been there, standing in the small shadowy room beside her. So near that she had only to turn to touch him—to feel the warmth of his skin under her hand...

She felt her whole body clench in a sudden shock of sheer yearning, and stopped, appalled at herself. What was the matter with her? How could she let her mind stray like this, in directions which should have been—and had to be—strictly taboo?

Just remember, she adjured herself savagely, that you're not alone. Exactly the same fantasies are probably being indulged in Athens and New York at this very moment—and they're only the ones you know about.

Xandreou's women, she thought with contempt, marching into the little shower-room, and turning on the water. She needed to cool off. To remember her pride and wash Nic Xandreou out of her mind and senses, she thought as she pulled off her clothes and stepped under the shower, lifting her face to the full force of the water.

She felt refreshed and more in control of her errant senses when she emerged, the enveloping towel anchored sarong-like just above her breasts, her hair hanging damply to her shoulders.

The rap on the bedroom door startled her. Katie was back sooner than she'd suspected. Judging by the way they'd had their heads together, she'd imagined that her sister and Arianna were on the beach for the duration, she thought drily as she opened the door.

But the smile died on her lips when she saw who was standing there.

It was Maria's nephew, the one who waited on tables. But out of uniform now—and out for mischief, her brain telegraphed the swift warning. The smile that slid over her was knowing—insolent, and she wished to God she were wearing more than just a wet towel.

She said curtly, 'Yes? What do you want?'

'I came to visit you, *thespinis*.' He peered past her. 'You are alone?'

'Yes, and I don't want company.' She tried to push the door shut, but he was too quick for her, shouldering his way into the room.

'Unless it's Nic Xandreou, *ne*? Tomorrow you go to him—live in his house—sleep in his bed. You thought no one would know?' The smile became a leer as he studied her shocked expression. 'Xandreou himself has told Kostas Philippides that you are leaving, and where you go.' His voice became insinuating. 'You should thank me, *thespinis*, for telling you where to find him.'

'You've already been thanked.' She was frightened now, but determined not to show it. 'Now get out before I tell your aunt.'

'You think she cares?' He laughed. 'She knows what you are. A little English whore to warm Xandreou's bed. But he is not the only man on Karthos.' He took a step nearer, the dark eyes hot and greedy on her bare shoulders and the first swell of her breasts above the towel. 'Who would know if I also tasted the honey Xandreou has chosen for himself?'

'I would know.' Nic Xandreou's voice was icily grim as he appeared with devastating suddenness in the doorway behind them. 'And also how to punish such a thief.'

'Kyrios Nicos.' The young Greek's swarthy skin was tinged with grey, and his tongue ran round his lips. 'I—I meant nothing. It was a joke...' He slid out into the passage, almost flattening himself into invisibility in his eagerness to escape.

Nic Xandreou followed, and Camilla heard the sound of a scuffle, a thud and a yelp of pain before he returned, rubbing his knuckles.

'You—hit him?' Camilla asked faintly.

Nic shrugged. 'He has a sore mouth,' he countered flatly. 'He will think before using it to insult another woman.'

'But nothing actually happened,' she protested, relief warring with mortification inside her.

'No thanks to you.' He looked her over, his brows snapping together ominously. 'Are you quite mad to permit such a one as that to enter your room—when you're unclothed? Or perhaps he was welcome.' His voice hardened. 'Maybe my own arrival was the real intrusion.'

'How dare you?' Camilla flared. 'You know that isn't true.'

'What do I know?' The dark eyes glittered at her as he put a wry hand to his cheek. 'You did not offer him the treatment you gave me.'

'I didn't get the chance,' Camilla said crossly. 'And I thought it was Katie at the door, or I'd never have opened it. I never dreamed it would be him—or that he'd think...' She halted, aware that she was blushing. 'Well, you heard him.'

'Yes.' He was silent for a moment. 'That was why I came back—to tell you that it might not be safe for you to remain here tonight. That there might be some form of harassment.'

'What made you think that?'

His mouth twisted. 'An absurdity. I thought—it was almost as if I heard you call out—cry for help.'

You did, Camilla thought with horror as she remembered how she'd conjured up his image, here in this room. But not in fear, she mused with a shiver.

'So I thought it best to return,' he went on. He gestured brusquely at the cases. 'Pack your things, *thespinis*, and come with me now. You cannot stay here any longer.'

She gasped. 'I'll have to fetch Katie. She's on the beach,' she added with a certain constraint, not wishing to mention Arianna's presence there too. Nic Xandreou would not approve of this newly hatched intimacy, she thought.

He frowned again. 'I will send Kostas to find her. And tell him too it is time he controlled his wife's relations, and became master in his own house,' he added harshly.

Camilla drew a breath. 'Isn't that rather a chauvinist viewpoint?'

'You can ask that—after what you have just experienced here?' His voice was hard.

'I'd say it in any circumstances,' Camilla hit back. 'And you don't seem to impose too many limitations on your own conduct,' she added shakily. 'It's thanks to you we're in this mess, after all. If you hadn't been so high-handed—and—mauled me in front of Maria, we'd be staying here. Instead we're moving to accommodation that belongs to you, and people will draw the obvious conclusion.'

'You will be there for a little less than two weeks,' he said tersely. 'Is that really so great a hardship?'

'Yes, it is.' She glared at him. 'When I know I'm going to be regarded as just another in a long line of—willing women,' she added bitterly.

Nic Xandreou took a swift harsh breath. 'No one,' he said. 'No one has ever dared speak to me as you do.'

'Then it's time someone did,' Camilla lifted her chin. 'Full time someone told you how—arrogant and unfeeling you are,' she added passionately, and burst, to her own consternation, into overwrought tears.

Nic Xandreou muttered some expletive half under his breath. Camilla found herself guided to the nearest bed, and seated on its edge, a handful of tissues from a box beside the bed pushed into her hand. Discovered, too, that her head was pressed against his shoulder, while his hand gently stroked her damp hair, and he murmured quietly and soothingly to her in his own language.

Self-consciously she drew away, scrubbing her face with the tissues. She mumbled, 'I'm sorry.'

'And I too regret—more than you can imagine,' he said with a touch of grimness. He put a hand under her chin, and lowered his mouth to hers. His lips were warm, almost gentle, but their touch was sensuous, bringing every pulse, every nerve-ending in her body to throbbing urgent life.

When he put her away from him, she could have cried out in disappointment. She stared up at him, watching his mouth slant in sardonic acknowledgement.

'Young Stavros was right,' he said. 'You are honey, *agape mou*. Honey and wine, and ripe, sweet fruit. All the things to tempt a man.' His fingers feathered delicately over her bare shoulder, and came to rest a brief millimetre away from the curve of her breast. 'But I,' he went on softly, 'am not in the market for such temptation. Especially as in two weeks you will be gone forever. I hope that reassures you.'

He kissed her again, the caress swift, hard, and carrying a kind of strange finality. Then he got up and went to the door.

Camilla watched it close behind him. Her skin was tingling where his hand had rested, and it hurt suddenly to breathe. It hurt...

I have to dress, she thought, swallowing past the pain. And I have to pack. Before he returns, and I have to go with him.

'Xandreou's woman'. That was what they would all think—all say as she left. It was a label which would haunt her until she left Karthos, and perhaps beyond.

And it isn't even true, she thought savagely—and was suddenly aware, with a shame that scorched her, that Nic Xandreou was not the only one with regrets.

CHAPTER SEVEN

IT WAS late afternoon when they arrived at the sea house. It had been a largely silent journey. Camilla, huddled on her side of the Jeep, had tried to concentrate on the scenery, which was spectacular enough to warrant it, and not Nic Xandreou's profile, which she found even more disturbing. And Katie was equally quiet, lost in her own thoughts.

Her first meeting with Nic had been formal on his side and composed on hers. She'd shown little of the hurt and indignation she must be feeling, and Camilla had felt both surprised and proud at her forbearance, and the maturity of her reaction.

On one side of the narrow pot-holed road, hillside covered in scrub soared upwards towards the unclouded arc of the sky to become, in time, a tall bleached mountain, all jagged silver and violet peaks and deep agate corries. High above them a solitary bird hovered, motionless and predatory.

On the other side, there was an almost sheer drop to the sea, sparkling like a brazen mirror under the sinking sun.

It seemed very remote, but wasn't that the idea? she thought bitterly. They were to be hidden away in this inaccessible place, and for

ₒotten there until their money ran out and they
were forced to leave.

Money, she thought with a stifled gasp of
distress. In the scramble to be ready she'd forgotten to get the money for their room back
from Kostas.

'There is something wrong?'

He didn't miss a thing.

She hunched a shoulder. 'No.' He was the
last person in the world who needed to know
they had a cash shortage. That would be
playing right into his hands. 'It's just—very
beautiful,' she added, gesturing around her.

He nodded. 'Every man sees his island as the
loveliest place on earth. I only wish I could
spend more time here, but our business interests are worldwide and expanding.'

He said it quite casually. Money, and the
power it bestowed, were things he took for
granted. And, with so much under his control,
the destinies of two young lovers would seem
an annoying triviality to be disposed of between one deal and the next. Spiro's and Katie's
happiness wouldn't feature on any of Nic
Xandreou's balance sheets.

That was something she needed to remember—to build up the flame of her anger
and resentment against him, and keep it
burning. She couldn't afford any more
weakness where he was concerned. No more
aching yearning to feel his mouth exploring
hers, or his hands spinning a web of sensual
delight on her skin.

The kind of spell he knew so well how to weave. The way he'd enthralled other fools.

But not me, she vowed with passion. Never again.

The Jeep swung off the road, and began to wind its way down a track so narrow that the shrubs and bushes which bordered it reached out to brush the sides of the vehicle. Pollen, heavy and golden, showered down on to Camilla's bare knee.

The Jeep turned a corner, and there in front of them, occupying its own headland, was the sea house. It was small by the standards of the Villa Apollo—single-storey, and roofed in faded terracotta tiles, their colour repeated in the shutters that hid the windows—and surrounded by a tangle of overgrown garden.

Camilla thought, It looks lonely, and instantly derided herself for being sentimental. Of course it was lonely—that was the whole point. They were being dumped in the back of beyond for the duration. She hadn't seen another hamlet, let alone a village within walking distance, during the entire journey.

Soula was waiting at the entrance as Nic brought the Jeep to a halt. She was small and plump, clad in the inevitable black dress and headscarf, but her wrinkled face was wreathed in smiles, as she took Camilla's hand in both of hers.

'Welcome,' she said. 'You are welcome, Kyria Camilla, and you too, Kyria Catherine.'

'I'm afraid we're causing a great deal of trouble,' Camilla said haltingly as Nic, his face set, unloaded their cases.

'No problem.' Soula gave a gusty sigh. 'At last life returns to this place.' She took both girls by the hand, tugging them forward. 'Come look.'

The house had been designed, Camilla realised, to capitalise on the views of the sea. Each room had its own superb vista, and the windows stood open to catch the breeze from the water, and the soft murmur of the waves.

A terrace had been built along the entire length of the house, overlooking the water, and from this a flight of steps led down, Soula told them, to a cove with a small sandy beach.

'Very private for the sun,' she added. 'Also good for swimming.'

The interior of the house was like walking straight into the heart of the sun. The floors were tiled in deep amber, the walls colour-washed in a paler shade of the same colour. The main living area was equipped with a sofa and several armchairs covered in a vibrant geometric print in shades of blue, gold and rust, with a separate raised dining area.

The room to which Camilla was shown opened directly on to the terrace, and was the largest of the bedrooms. She looked around slowly, assimilating the patina of the wood of the built-in furniture, and the enormous wall-hanging in rich earthy shades of bronze, copper and gold which supplied a dramatic background to the wide bed with its linen the colour of warm cream.

'You like?' Soula demanded anxiously.

'Like' was hardly the word, Camilla thought, drawing a breath. She said, 'It's—magnificent.'

Soula nodded her satisfaction, missing the touch of uncertainty in Camilla's voice. 'I bring you coffee,' she said. 'Kyria Catherine will rest until dinner. She has a little headache, I think.'

No, Camilla thought with an inward sigh. She has one enormous headache, which I share.

This had to be the master bedroom, she told herself tautly, when she was alone. This was where Nic Xandreou had brought his bride. And in that bed he'd made her his wife.

For a moment her mind ran riot, then she closed off the clamorous, disturbing images, her nails scoring the soft palms of her hands. Well, she couldn't—wouldn't sleep there. She'd swap with Katie, on whom all the implications of the room would be lost.

She felt stifled suddenly, and headed for the windows, pushing open the shutters as she sought the fresh air of the terrace.

But under the heavy canopy of bougainvillaea she paused.

Because he was there, she realised tautly, seated on the low parapet, his figure darkly silhouetted against the glitter of the sea, as he stared out at the horizon.

As if some silent signal had alerted him to her presence, he turned his head and looked at her, his expression starkly, almost bitterly arrested.

She knew of course what he must be seeing—another girl emerging from the room they had once shared, standing for a moment, framed by flowers. That girl would have smiled, evoking memories of the night that had just passed, promising more pleasure to come. She would have held out her hands—walked across the terrace, and into his arms.

They said time healed, she thought, but judging by his face Nic Xandreou's bereavement must have inflicted a wound as deep as the whispering sea around them.

She moved hurriedly away from the bedroom window, and its connotations, forcing a smile, hastening into speech to conceal her own sudden pain.

'I can see why it's called the sea house.'

He nodded. 'My father built it. He loved the sea, and always kept a caique moored in the cove below. Later, when Arianna and Spiro were born, he sold our house in Karthos town, and started on the Villa Apollo. But this place was always a refuge for him—for all of us.' His fleeting smile mocked her. 'Quite separate from the main house.' He pointed across the small bay to the adjoining headland and to where the sun highlighted white walls amid a cluster of encircling greenery. 'Which is there.'

'So close?' Camilla was taken aback. 'I—I didn't realise.'

'But only by sea,' he said laconically. 'There is no direct road between the two properties. One must go a considerable way inland, as you must have realised, and this has proved an inconvenience—in the past.' His brief pause told her the present was a different matter.

He picked a loose stone off the parapet, and tossed it down into the rippling dark blue water. 'Spiro and I used to swim from one house to another,' he went on almost musingly. A faint smile twisted his mouth. 'How strong a swimmer are you, Camilla?'

'Good enough,' she said shortly. 'But not so expert as to risk that distance.'

'I'm glad you are so conscious of your safety.' His smile widened, mocking her. 'It is always best, I think, to know one's limitations, and abide by them,' he added silkily.

'Oh, I've got the picture.' Camilla glanced round. 'Here we are, and here we'll stay. Isn't that it?'

'You are hardly prisoners,' he said sardonically. 'You are free to leave whenever you wish.'

'But on whose terms?' Camilla met his glance levelly.

He laughed. 'Again, I am sure you have the picture.' He paused. 'You should at least listen to my offer, Camilla. I am prepared to be generous—within reason.'

Camilla shook her head. 'No deal.'

'I am sure that is not your final word.' Nic's voice was silky. 'Here you will have leisure and

tranquillity to think. And when you are ready
to talk, you have only to let me know.'

'You'll wait a long time,' she said tersely.

'But I think my resources will outlast yours.'
He paused again. 'Which reminds me.' He
reached for his jacket, flung across the parapet
beside him, and extracted a bulky envelope
from an inside pocket. 'This is for you.'

The envelope was crammed with Greek
drachmae in a variety of denominations.
Camilla thrust it back at him. 'What is this?
A down-payment on my ultimate co-operation?
No way, Mr Xandreou.'

'Actually, the money is yours, Kyria Dryden.'
His tone jeered at her own formality. 'The
refund on your hotel room. Fortunately Kostas
has a conscience as well as a bitch of a wife.'
He closed her fingers round the envelope, and,
despite herself, a swift burning tingle ran up
her arm at the brush of his hand on hers. 'Take
it,' he urged softly. 'You will need all the cash
you can get if you seriously mean to prolong
this battle between us.'

She looked down at the envelope. 'You didn't
have to hand it over. You'd be quite entitled to
keep it—as rent.'

The dark eyes flashed. 'Please do not insult
me by such a suggestion,' he said. 'You are my
guest here—you and your sister.'

'But I'd rather we paid our way,' she said
stubbornly. 'You—you can't pretend we're
welcome here.'

'Perhaps not, but it provides an opportunity to settle matters between us before you go home.'

She took a breath. 'You're really so sure you'll win?' she said bitterly.

'Oh, yes.' His voice was soft. 'One way or another.'

His glance seemed to touch her, lingering on her mouth, then sweeping down to the swell of her breasts, reminding her that his most lethal armament in this conflict was his virile, charismatic sexuality.

Whereas she had nothing to fight with but her own convictions and determination. Could they ever be enough?

Nic lifted himself lithely from the parapet, glancing at his watch. 'I must get back, I'm expecting a call from New York.'

'A personal call?' some demon prompted her to ask.

His mouth twisted. 'My sister has been busy,' he commented with a touch of grimness. 'But I don't think, *matia mou*, that is any concern of yours.' He paused. 'Think about what I have said, and remember I am prepared to reopen negotiations at any time.'

'I'll negotiate,' she said steadily. 'But only on condition that you let Katie see Spiro. Can't you see that she might be able to jog his memory? Isn't it at least worth trying—to have him cured—restored to the way he used to be with no blank spots in his mind?'

His face hardened. 'Spiro will recover in time. And if there are blanks——' he shrugged '—well, your sister's intervention in his life is best forgotten anyway.'

'That's cruel.' Camilla's voice shook.

'It is also practical.' His smile held no amusement. 'When you realise, finally, that you do not make conditions, you will be free to concentrate solely on the terms of our eventual bargain. There is no other real alternative, I promise you.'

He absorbed, with irony, the stricken look on her face. 'And now I wish you goodnight, Camilla.' The dark eyes glittered at her. 'Sleep well in my bed, *agape mou*—if you can.'

He inclined his head to her almost formally, and was gone, his parting words smarting like the lash of a whip across her consciousness.

'No problem,' Katie said cheerfully, tucking into her helping of Soula's delicious chicken in lemon sauce that evening.

Camilla stared at her. 'I wish I shared your confidence,' she said wearily. 'We're here, and Spiro might as well be at the end of the universe.'

Katie shook her head. 'He's not that far away,' she said firmly. 'Arianna says we must just be patient for a while—bide our time.'

'Really?' Camilla queried drily. 'Just remember, darling, that Arianna's a Xandreou as well. And it was her idea to strand us here, out of harm's way. Are you quite sure you can trust her?'

'Absolutely. Nic's trying to rule her life too—push her into marrying a man she doesn't love.'

'Oh.' Camilla digested this. 'And Arianna presumably has other plans?'

'Of course,' Katie said serenely. 'She's in love with Petros—Dr Deroulades.'

'My God,' Camilla said faintly. The young doctor seemed the unlikeliest of targets for someone as glamorous and worldly as Arianna. Yet there was great kindness in his face, she thought slowly, and integrity in the gaze behind his spectacles.

I knew she was up to something, she thought, but not this.

'And he loves her too,' Katie went on. 'They've known each other all their lives. In fact the Xandreou family paid for Petros's medical training. But he's not rich or powerful, of course, so Nic wouldn't even consider him as a suitable husband for Arianna.' She sighed. 'Arianna says if he had the least idea they were in love he would be terribly angry. Petros would lose his job at the clinic and be sent away from Karthos altogether, and she would never see him again. And Nic's vengeance would follow him wherever he went,' she added.

'I can imagine,' Camilla said grimly.

Katie pushed away her empty plate. 'So, they have to pretend when they meet in public, and see each other properly in secret.'

'She told you all this today?' Camilla asked, frowning.

Katie nodded. 'It's a mutual pact,' she said. 'She helps reunite me with Spiro, we do what we can for Arianna and Petros in return.'

'I don't like the sound of this.' Camilla shook her head. 'We have enough problems already. And Nic Xandreou may actually have a point,' she added grudgingly. 'Arianna seems an expensive proposition for someone on a doctor's salary. Maybe she needs a convenient millionaire.'

'Camilla.' Katie was shocked. 'You're surely not on *his* side?'

'I'm not taking sides,' Camilla said defensively. 'Just trying to be realistic. If we interfere, we could have Nic Xandreou's vengeance following us as well, and we don't need that.'

'You forget,' Katie said gently. 'We'll have Spiro to protect us.' Her eyes shone. 'Everything's going to be fine. I know it.'

Camilla could find nothing to say in the face of such sincere and passionate conviction.

Later, alone in her room, she found herself hoping that Katie was right—about all of it.

She looked around her with dissatisfaction. Her plan to swap accommodation with Katie had been forestalled firstly by Soula who had unpacked for her, and put all her things away. Any attempt at change now would inevitably become some kind of big deal, and might even get to the ears of Nic Xandreou, who would draw his own all too accurate conclusions.

And I don't need that, she muttered to herself.

And then Katie had disclosed, starry-eyed, that she could see the lights from the Villa Apollo from her window, which made her feel that Spiro was close to her.

And after that, of course, there was nothing more to be said.

I shall have to bear it, Camilla thought. Even if I can't manage the usual grin.

She took the passports and the envelope of money Nic had given her, and looked round for a safe place to put them. The drawer in the night-table beside the bed seemed the obvious repository, but that was easier said than done, she realised with vexation, when the drawer refused to budge.

At first, she thought it might be locked, then she realised that something bulky had been put into the drawer and become wedged. After some manoeuvring with her steel comb, she managed to free the obstruction, and open the drawer.

She found herself holding a photograph in an ornate but tarnished silver frame.

It was the picture of a girl, the face radiant, almost flawlessly beautiful. Blonde hair tumbling on to bare shoulders. Full lips parting in a smile to reveal perfect teeth. Violet eyes, glowing a provocative invitation.

And all of it oddly but elusively familiar, Camilla thought wonderingly.

There was a scrawl of writing across the bottom left-hand corner. The words seemed to leap up at her. 'To Nic, on our wedding-day. Forever, Rachelle.'

Camilla drew a sharp breath. Of course, she thought. It was Rachelle Morgan, the actress. She'd blazed across the cinema world in a brief, stormy career, which had included an Oscar nomination as well as rows with leading men, and an eventual sacking from a film. She'd never made another, and Camilla remembered reading some years before of her death from a drugs overdose in some Los Angeles motel.

She sank down on the edge of the bed. This—*this* was the girl Nic Xandreou had married, she thought faintly. A far cry from the docile Greek heiress of her imagination. And clearly a very different marriage from the ideal he'd outlined to her. Perhaps she could now understand, if not condone, his reasons.

Rachelle Morgan had died alone a long way from Karthos, and the sea pavilion. In fact, Camilla could recall in all the attendant publicity about her career no mention of any marriage, or any husband left to mourn in the tragic aftermath.

No wonder Nic was bitter, nor that the scars of his loss had gone so deep.

For him, 'forever' had been over too soon. If it had even existed at all ...

Nic Xandreou was no all-conquering god. Just a man, as Arianna had said, who'd been burned and now feared the fire in consequence.

Or was it Rachelle Morgan who'd been scorched instead? The thought struck her like a blow from a clenched fist. Had she, like some latter-day Icarus, flown too near the Xandreou sun, not comprehending its power, only to drop like a stone to earth in the ruin of her wings?

Who could say what demons had driven all that beauty and talent to destruction?

Hands shaking, Camilla put the photograph down beside her bed. She would keep it there, she thought, shivering, as a timely reminder. A warning even.

She felt suddenly cold. 'Dear God,' she whispered. 'He could destroy me too—so very easily.'

CHAPTER EIGHT

SLEEP did not come easily to Camilla that night. Huddled awkwardly under a single sheet at the edge of the bed, she found her search for temporary oblivion distorted and disturbed by unwanted thoughts and images which even pursued her into her dreams.

A tall man with skin like bronze, and eyes like a dark flame, moved through those dreams, lay beside her, shared her pillow.

She could feel the warmth of his body against hers, the fever of his lips, the frank enticement of his hands as they explored her. Found herself reaching out in turn, seeking him vainly in the still heat of the night. Only to realise, with a frightening sense of desolation, that she was alone.

She drew an angry breath, kicking away the imprisoning tangle of sheet from her over-heated body. What was happening to her? How could she possibly feel these things about a man who was still virtually a stranger, and almost certainly an enemy?

'Damn you, Nic Xandreou,' she whispered into the darkness. 'I should never have come here, and now I'm trapped, and I can't get away.'

She escaped at last into a restless doze, only to be jolted back into wakefulness again by the certainty that she could hear something—someone moving on the terrace outside.

She sat up, pushing the hair back from her face, staring towards the shuttered windows, her heart thumping erratically. She'd thought the sea house too remote for intruders, but now...

She swung her feet to the floor, reaching for the white cotton peignoir trimmed with broderie anglaise which matched her nightgown.

The early morning air was fresh as she stepped out on to the terrace. The sky was pale, almost misty. The sea was a ripple of silver. A faint breeze stirred in the bougainvillaea above her head. There was no one there, of course, and yet...

'Kalimera.'

Camilla whirled with a startled cry. Nic Xandreou was standing, hands on hips, a few yards away outside the open window of the saloni from which he'd obviously just emerged.

He was wearing ancient denim jeans, hacked off at mid-thigh, and a short-sleeved black shirt, unbuttoned almost to the waist. He looked tough, virile, and devastatingly sexy—last night's dream come suddenly alive in front of her.

Remembering the precise nature of that dream, Camilla found colour mounting in her face, and her hand went to her throat to clutch the edges of her peignoir more tightly together.

'You!' she said unevenly. 'What are you doing here?'

His brows lifted, the amusedly cynical appraisal of his dark eyes telling her that neither the blush or the betrayingly defensive gesture had been lost on him.

'This is my property,' he reminded her drily.

'But you never come here,' she protested, then caught herself. 'At least . . .'

'That is what Arianna told you,' he supplied. 'She exaggerates. I come to visit Soula, naturally.'

'At this hour?' Camilla glanced at her watch.

'No, this morning I've been fishing so there will be fresh mullet for your dinner tonight.'

She said blankly, 'I don't believe it.'

Nic shrugged. 'The proof is in the kitchen. Do you wish to look?'

'No—I mean—I can't see you as a simple fisherman, alone in the dawn.'

He laughed. 'Yet to a Greek the sea is like the blood in his veins. And on a boat you have time to be alone—to think. Often, it's the only time.'

'A boat?' Camilla parodied astonishment. 'I thought you had your own shipping line.'

'I do,' he said silkily. 'But that is not the same thing at all. Like my father before me, I keep a caique for my own use.' He paused. 'However, I did not intend my visit to wake you. I apologise.'

She bit her lip. 'It doesn't matter. I didn't have a particularly good night, anyway.'

'No?' The dark eyes mocked her.

'No,' she returned tautly. 'This isn't exactly an easy situation—for any of us.'

Nic shrugged again. 'You can resolve it any time you wish,' he retorted.

'You mean—take the money and go.' She lifted her chin. 'Never.'

'That will not be your final decision,' he said. 'I can wait.'

'It isn't my decision to make—or yours. Spiro and Katie are the people concerned—or should be.'

'Unfortunately such sentimental notions have no place in real life.' He sounded bored.

'And what do you know about "real life", Mr Xandreou, shut up in your ivory tower of power and money?' Camilla's voice had an edge. 'You only have to wish for something and it's granted—snap your fingers, and everyone dashes to obey.'

'Naturally you exclude yourself from this fascinating picture of mass acquiescence,' Nic said grimly.

'Of course. You can't expect to own the whole world.'

'I've never wanted to.' His tone hardened. 'Once I thought, as you seem to do, that love could conquer all barriers. But not any longer. A collision between two different worlds can lead only to disaster.' His face was brooding, bitterly introspective, as he looked around him.

'This is a lesson I was forced to learn with the kind of pain I would wish on no one—least of all my young brother.'

'But you can't protect him from experience—or prevent him making his own mistakes,' Camilla protested. 'It doesn't work like that.'

'So you admit that Spiro and your sister would be a mistake.'

'No,' she said wearily. 'I'm trying to say that you and I aren't qualified to make judgements for them.' She took a deep breath. 'It's terrible—a tragedy that your marriage ended as it did—that someone so lovely, with so much going for her——' her voice faltered a little '—should be simply wiped out, but Katie and Spiro are still entitled to lead their own lives, whatever the cost.'

Nic Xandreou was very still, his tall figure suddenly menacing in the clear morning light.

'What do you know of my marriage?'

'Nothing at all, really.' She swallowed. 'But—but I found your wife's photograph, and realised who she was.'

'What are you saying?' His face was thunderous. 'Show me.'

Camilla turned and went back into the bedroom, uneasily aware that he was following. She picked up the photograph and handed it to him. 'It was in this drawer. It must have been pushed in there and forgotten.'

He said harshly, 'An unforgivable oversight. I gave orders for everything to be removed. I

wanted nothing left here to remind me.' The
dark eyes looked around him, taking in the
disordered bed, the intimate clutter of Camilla's
toiletries, and discarded clothes. 'Nothing,' he
repeated slowly.

Her voice shook a little. 'But you can't easily
forget—beauty like hers.'

'Yet you can try.' His mouth was set. He took
the backing from the frame, which he tossed
contemptuously aside, then ripped the print
across, again and again, letting the torn fragments flutter to the floor.

Camilla gave a small distressed cry. 'Oh, no.
Oh, how could you?'

'It was simple, believe me.' He swung back
to her, his smile almost a snarl. 'This—this is
the complication.'

His hands were hard on her shoulders as he
pulled her towards him. Her startled eyes read
the purpose in his face, but even as her lips
framed a negation his mouth possessed hers,
making no concession in its fierce demand. The
scent of his skin, fragrant with sunlight and
the sea, seemed to invade her senses—to fill
her being with a harsh and undeniable longing.

She found she was kissing him in return with
the same vibrant, consuming urgency, her lips
parting eagerly to accept the thrust of his
tongue.

Pinned against his body, she was aware of
every bone, muscle and sinew in his taut, virile
frame. Could feel the heat and strength of his
arousal, mirroring the rising flame inside her.

Nic's hand shook as he pulled apart the ribbons of the peignoir, allowing his lips to traverse the vulnerable line of her throat, and the curve of her shoulder. His fingers slid under the strap of her nightgown, tugging it down, baring one rose-tipped breast to his caress.

His palm cupped the soft mound, his thumb brushing the tautening peak, piercing her with a shaft of bewildered pleasure bordering on pain.

The dark head bent to her, and he took the small engorged bud into his mouth, laving it with his tongue, his mouth like fire against her skin. She felt her body judder in anguished delight, her hands lifting to twist in the thick, crisp hair at the nape of his neck.

He lifted her on to the bed, and lay beside her. She was caught in the dream again, she thought dazedly, fright and excitement warring for mastery inside her.

She was sinking down into the softness of the mattress, the weight of his lean body imprisoning her, creating new hungers in every trembling inch of her as she strained towards him in this new and incomprehensible desperation.

He pushed down the other strap of her nightgown, his face absorbed, intent, his mouth hot and seeking against her fragrant flesh. His hands were urgent as they stroked her body through the thin fabric, pushing its hem up towards her thigh with swift and sensual purpose.

'*Se thelo.*' His voice was husky against the uneven beat of her heart. '*Se thelo poli.*'

And the alien words which instinct warned her spoke only of physical need, and no warmer, tenderer emotion, sent the dream shattering into sudden, cold reality.

She was insane, she thought with fear. She must be—lying here on the bed he'd once shared with his wife—a girl whose promise-filled life had ended in isolation and despair. Whose torn photograph was scattered at their feet in ultimate rejection.

And she was letting him touch her—oh, God—letting him *use* her like some sensual exorcism.

She braced her hands against his chest, pushing him away, her body rigid with panic and denial.

'*Matia mou*—what is it? What's wrong?'

'Everything,' Camilla said hoarsely. 'Let go of me—leave me alone. How—how dare you...?'

She scrambled off the bed, dragging the bodice of the nightdress up to cover her breasts, her hands clumsy with shame and remorse.

Nic lifted himself on to an elbow and observed her struggles, his eyes hooded, his firm mouth twisting cynically.

'There was no question of daring, *agape mou*. You wanted what was happening as much as I did. Perhaps more,' he added with swift, silky cruelty.

Camilla gasped, mortified colour burning her face. She said unsteadily, 'Get out of this room. Get away from me.'

'Are you sure?' There was deliberate insolence in his voice—in the look which raked her—stripped her. 'Perhaps you should learn to be more accommodating—like your sister. You might find there was more to be gained. That, in certain circumstances, I could be persuaded to be generous.'

She flung back her head. 'Become just another "Xandreou's woman"?' Her voice was uneven. 'You over-estimate your attractions, *kyrie*. I'd beg in the streets first.'

Nic's eyes narrowed, but he shrugged as he swung himself off the bed. 'That is your choice, of course. But I should warn you there is a time limit to the terms I'm prepared to offer—all of them.' He paused to allow the implication in his words to sink in. 'Maybe it would be wiser, for your sister's sake, to think again—and soon.'

He walked without haste to the open window, turning to touch his fingertips to his lips in a parody of a tender farewell.

He said softly, 'Send me word when you have changed your mind.'

'About what?' Camilla demanded tautly.

His eyes swept her body again, and he smiled. 'Everything,' he said, and was gone.

It was another flawless morning, baking hot already, even under the protection of a sun umbrella. Camilla, ensconced on a lounger in a sheltered part of the terrace, could hear the sound of voices from the *saloni*, and guessed that Arianna had arrived for her daily visit.

Her misgivings about the Greek girl had been unjustified, she was bound to admit. Her presence at the sea house was, for Katie, a much needed link with Spiro, and also the outside world as the sea house had no phone.

Three endless days had dragged by since that devastating encounter with Nic, and, although there had been neither sight nor sound of him since, her emotions were still ragged, her senses in turmoil.

She had told herself a hundred times that this crazy, unwanted infatuation with Nic Xandreou—for that was all it was, all it ever could be—meant nothing. Absolutely and finally nothing.

Life in England might not have been easy, but she'd coped—earned herself a reputation for being calm and reliable. Yet now...

I don't know what's happening to me, she thought desperately. I'm not in control any more, and I hate it. I miss my peace of mind. I want it back.

But there would be no inner tranquillity for her on Karthos. Living in the sea house was a constant torment, with its reminders of the shadowed past Nic had shared there with his beautiful young wife—and those even more potent recent memories, from which there was no escape.

The thought of his lovemaking still seared her skin. His presence seemed to linger in the room, evoking a strange trembling awareness she had no power to suppress.

Soula had cleared up the torn fragments of the photograph, her plump face sad, her mouth discreetly compressed. Her employer's marriage was a subject on which she was clearly not prepared to be drawn, although she would chat to Katie by the hour about the old days when both Nic Xandreou and his brother were boys.

Arianna had explained the situation to her, and she had taken Katie firmly under her wing, supervising her diet, and rationing her hours in the sun.

As for Nic himself, presumably he was staying aloof, awaiting her message to say she was ready to deal, Camilla thought bitterly.

But, even when he was absent, she was always aware of him, just the same. Sometimes, across the shimmering water, the Villa Apollo looked almost close enough to touch, and as she sunbathed or swam in the shallow waters of the cove she had the odd impression that unseen eyes were watching her, although she knew that was absurd.

The need to go—to get away before it was too late—had begun to obsess her. Part of her mind was saying that her mission to Karthos was hopeless, anyway. That maybe Nic did hold all the aces, and their best course would be to agree to some kind of financial settlement. But she knew any suggestion to Katie they should cut their losses and return to England would be indignantly resisted.

Katie, immersed in her own emotional maelstrom, had no idea of the confusion that was ripping her sister apart. Nor did Camilla want her to know.

'*Kalimera.*' Arianna appeared beside her, looking cool and elegant in a slim-fitting dress the colour of peppermint ice. 'Soula insists your sister must rest on her bed a little.'

'She's been very kind,' Camilla said rather stiltedly.

Arianna shrugged. 'She loves Spiro, and wants to see him happy. But how to achieve it, that is the problem.' She sat down on an adjoining lounger. 'Petros has promised he will bring Katie and Spiro together as soon as the coast is clear.'

She spread her hands. 'But Nicos is rarely away from the Villa Apollo these days, and when he is absent it is only for a short time—and he leaves Yannis to watch Spiro.' She frowned. 'We must find some way of drawing him from the villa, and keeping him away for several hours.'

Camilla said constrictedly, 'Surely he'll be going to Athens some time...'

'You mean to see Zoe?' Arianna gave a worldly shrug. 'Who knows? Nicos does not discuss such things with me, and he is too concerned with Spiro anyway. In fact——' she leaned forward '—he has told Petros that he may soon take Spiro to the States to see specialists there, and if he does...' she shrugged again ' ... I think that will be the end of your hopes. You could not afford to follow him there.'

'No,' Camilla said quietly. 'We couldn't. Does Katie know about this?'

'No. I thought it best to say nothing. But,' Arianna said briskly, 'it means there is no time to be lost. We must make a diversion somehow for Nicos. Get him away from the villa for half a day—a day even.' Her brilliant gaze switched to Camilla. 'This will be your task, I think.'

'Minc?' Camilla sat bolt upright on her lounger. 'What are you talking about?'

Arianna's smile was oblique. 'You tell Nicos you wish to meet with him, to make a deal, but away from here so that your sister will not know and be upset. And then you keep him with you,' she added, her smile widening. 'It will be no problem. He is an attractive man, *ne*, and you—intrigue him, I think.'

'No.' Bright spots of colour burned in Camilla's face. 'I'm sorry, but I can't—I won't. It's quite impossible.' Her heart was thumping against her ribcage. 'Anyway he wouldn't believe me. I've made it more than clear that I won't negotiate.'

'But isn't it also a woman's privilege to change her mind?' Arianna asked. 'That is something Nicos understands very well, I think.'

Camilla sank her teeth into her lower lip. 'I'm—sure he does. But I don't play those kinds of games.'

Arianna shrugged again, this time with an air of fatalism. 'Then we can do nothing. Spiro will go to America, and you will go home with a suntan and some money.'

Camilla groaned inwardly.

'I'd never get away with it,' she said desperately.

'Unless you try, how can you know?' Arianna demanded. 'Besides, Nicos has always said that an easy deal is one not worth making. He expects a fight.' Her eyes gleamed at Camilla. 'But not always the choice of battle-field—or weapons.'

There was a loaded silence.

At last Camilla said helplessly, 'All right— I'll try, but I'm not promising a thing.'

'Good,' Arianna approved with the familiar cat-like grin. 'Because now you could have the perfect opportunity.' She pointed a pink-tipped finger. 'My brother comes here, I think.'

Camilla saw that a blue boat, its tan sail neatly furled, had come round the adjoining headland, and was making for the cove.

'Oh, God.' The breath seemed to choke in her throat. She turned on Arianna. 'You knew already—didn't you?' she accused. 'That he was coming here. You've set me up.'

'No, I swear it. He said nothing at breakfast. But it is a chance we cannot miss, *ne*?' she went on pleadingly. 'For the sake of Spiro and your sister, tell him you wish to talk to him privately. Make him take you with him on the boat, wherever he is going—then keep him with you until the sun has set. Give us time.'

She rose gracefully to her feet. 'As soon as you have left with him, I will take Katie to the clinic to fetch Petros so that he may supervise their meeting, then we will all go straight to the Villa Apollo.' She put her cheek swiftly against Camilla's. 'Good luck to us all,' she whispered, and was gone in a cloud of warm fragrance.

Camilla looked at the approaching boat, and the dark figure at the tiller, then at the brilliant sky.

It would be a very long time until sunset, she realised numbly. And she would need more than luck to come through unscathed.

She said aloud, softly and despairingly, 'Oh, God, what have I just agreed to?'

CHAPTER NINE

CAMILLA waited for him on the small wooden jetty built out from the beach, standing slim and straight in the sleeveless, button-through sundress, with its deep scooped neck, which matched, and now covered, her jade-green bikini. Chin tilted slightly to conceal her nervousness, she watched him bring *Calliope* expertly alongside.

'*Kalimera*.' He tossed a rope to her, then swung himself lithely ashore. He was wearing brief white shorts which hugged his lean hips, topped by a sea-island cotton shirt striped in red and navy. 'I hope I haven't kept you waiting.'

'I wasn't aware that I'd sent for you,' she retorted, and caught herself. That wasn't the persuasive note Arianna had suggested.

He shrugged. 'But I knew it would only be a matter of time.' He was half smiling, the dark eyes narrowed and speculative.

'How?'

'Because whatever wrongs you feel your sister has suffered, you have to go back,' he said. 'You have a life to return to—a job which you need because times are hard.' His glance travelled with cool deliberation down her body. 'Maybe even a man.'

The inflexion in his voice made it a question rather than a statement.

'That,' Camilla said quietly, 'is none of your business.'

'Then let us discuss the real business between us. That is why you are here, *ne*? Because you are ready to negotiate a settlement?'

'I—I don't seem to have a choice.' Camilla avoided the intensity of his gaze.

'At last you see reason.' There was satisfaction in his tone. 'I will call on you this evening after dinner with details of my proposals.'

'Oh, no.' That was the wrong plan altogether, Camilla thought with alarm. 'I mean—I'd hoped to talk things over with you—privately, first—before I break the news to my sister.'

He shrugged. 'Very well—when?'

Camilla took a deep breath. 'There's no time like the present.'

'Now?' The dark brows lifted. 'That is not possible. I have only called to see Soula, to pay her some money for the house. Then I am going to Marynthos, a village on the other side of the island.'

Camilla's nails dug into the palms of her hands. 'Couldn't I come with you?' She saw a flare of surprise in his face and hurried on. 'Now that I've made up my mind, I don't want to let things—drag on. And, anyway, I've hardly seen anything of Karthos, and this could be my last chance. That is if you don't mind a passenger,' she added, challenging his lengthening silence.

'No,' he said at last, his smile crooked. 'I do not—mind. But you, *matia mou*—are you prepared to take the risk?'

'Risk?' Camilla glanced around her and shrugged. 'The weather seems set fair, and I'm a good sailor anyway.'

'That is not,' Nic said quite gently, 'what I meant.' As their eyes met, a faint shiver went through her, mingling fear and excitement. He laughed suddenly, and held out a hand to help her into the caique. '*Ela tora*. Come on, then, Kyria Camilla.'

So far, so good, Camilla told herself as he manoeuvred the boat away from the jetty and turned the bow towards the open sea. She risked one fleeting glance back at the sea house. Which, of course, he saw.

'Should you have left a message for your sister? Will she be concerned?'

'Katie's resting,' she said briefly. 'And I mentioned I might go out today—find out what the island has to offer.'

'Then I shall have to make sure you are not disappointed.' There was a vein of amusement underlying the courteous words that wasn't lost on her.

He thought she was a pushover, she realised with a swift smart of shame. That she'd come with him for a brief sexual adventure, although that was what she needed him to think, of course. She had to use all that superb male

confidence against him, to bolster her own resolve not to fall into that sensual, charismatic
web he knew so well how to weave, and become
just another of Xandreou's women.

I'll be the one that got away, she assured
herself. Oh, God, I've got to be...

'Would you like to steer?' His voice broke
across her uncomfortable reverie.

'Is it safe?' she asked doubtfully, and Nic
laughed.

'I won't let you sink us, *matia mou.*'

'Why do you call me that? What does it
mean?' Camilla asked as she gingerly took the
tiller.

'It means "my eyes",' Nic said, after a
pause. 'When a woman allows a man to look
into her eyes, Camilla *mou*, she offers him a
key to the secrets of her heart.' He paused. 'Or
so it is said.'

Her pulses quickened. She said flippantly,
'No wonder so many people wear sunglasses,
in that case.'

'You do not.'

'Well.' Camilla shrugged. 'Perhaps I have
nothing to hide.'

'No?' He took her chin in his hand, turning
her gently but inexorably to face him. For a
startled moment, she found his dark gaze
burning into hers. 'I see anger, Camilla, and
defiance, and anxiety, and behind these a
mystery as deep as the sea.' He paused again.
'What I have never seen is laughter.'

'That's hardly surprising.' She freed herself with a swift jerk of her head. 'After all, I haven't found a great deal to laugh about since I got here.'

'Or before that, either, I think.' His voice was reflective. 'How long have you had the sole responsibility for your sister?'

'Three—nearly four years.' Her voice shook as she told him briefly about the accident. 'But—please,' she added hurriedly, 'you mustn't think it's been some kind of burden. Katie's a wonderful girl. She's never given me a moment's worry...' She stopped, feeling foolish.

'Until now,' he said drily.

Camilla shrugged. 'I didn't bargain for her falling in love.'

'No?' His smile was faintly cynical. 'Have you forgotten the power of a warm night under the moon?'

'No.' She wouldn't admit that she'd never experienced it. 'I just thought Katie was more—level-headed, that's all.'

She needed to find a less personal topic—defer any discussion about Katie for as long as possible, she reminded herself.

'Why are we going to Marynthos?' she asked brightly. 'Is there something special there?'

'Very special—a new baby—the son of my friend Dimitris Ioannides. He's asked me to be godfather.'

'And you've agreed?' She couldn't hide her surprise.

'Of course,' he said with slight hauteur. 'We Greeks take such a responsibility very seriously.'

'Oh.' Camilla swallowed. 'I didn't realise I'd be intruding on such a private occasion. I'm sorry.'

'If I thought you would intrude, you would not be here.' His tone was matter-of-fact.

'Oh.' She could easily, she realised, have been left standing on the jetty. 'Thank you—I think.'

'*Parakalo*.' His grin was swift, and oblique. His hand covered hers on the tiller. 'You have strayed a little off course,' he cautioned. 'Take care.'

Yes, Camilla thought grimly, feeling her flesh warm and tingle at the contact with his. I certainly will.

She removed her own hand, and said coolly, 'Perhaps you'd better take over. I don't want to end up on the rocks.'

'As you wish. Relax, then, and enjoy the trip. Feel the sun on your face.' He reached out and released the barrette which confined her hair at the nape of her neck. 'And the wind in your hair,' he added, tossing the barrette casually overboard.

'Why the hell did you do that?' Camilla demanded furiously, trying to control her chestnut mane with her fingers, and failing as the breeze gleefully whipped it into a tangle.

'Because today, *agape mou*,' Nic drawled, 'you are not the tied-back, buttoned-up, oh, so responsible sister. She is consigned to the oblivion she deserves. Today you will drink wine and taste life.' He paused. 'And your eyes will smile at me. Is it agreed?'

Camilla looked down at the vivid sea, sparkling and dancing round the boat, feeling its restless excitement thrill suddenly through her own veins.

Today. The thought was like a prayer to placate the ancient envious gods. One day out of all eternity. Was it so much to ask?

She flung back her head recklessly. 'Agreed,' she said.

An hour later, they reached Marynthos. It was only a small village—a straggle of white buildings with coloured roofs round a natural inlet where fishing boats bobbed. And a welcoming committee, Camilla noted, with an inrush of shyness.

She said, 'Shall I stay on *Calliope*?'

'By no means. Dimitris would be most offended if you failed to admire his son.'

He took her arm, urging her on to the narrow quay, responding to the noisy babble of greetings, putting names unerringly to the crowd of smiling faces which surged round them.

They were almost lifted off their feet on a wave of goodwill which carried them up the steep and narrow street. Here the women were waiting more decorously, the youngest children playing in the dust at their feet. The two grandmothers, wearing the inevitable black dresses and headscarves, offered a formal welcome, and then Dimitris Ioannides himself appeared, a neat, bright-eyed man, his teeth gleaming in a grin of pure delight under his heavy moustache.

The two men shook hands, then embraced, slapping each other on the back. Then Nic beckoned Camilla forward.

Her hand was taken and held for a moment by Dimitris. 'Welcome,' he said in careful English. 'You are welcome, *thespinis*.'

She was given a glass of wine, heavy and rather sweet, made, Nic told her, from Dimitris's own grapes, then was conducted into the house to see the baby.

Hara Ioannides was sitting up in bed, holding him in her arms. She was a pretty girl, her face wearily contented as she crooned to her child.

She greeted Nic shyly but with composure, and put the baby into his arms amid applause from the rest of the family clustering in the doorway.

Clearly a visit from such an important and respected figure as Nic Xandreou was an event in their lives, Camilla realised. The fact that he had agreed to be godfather was an additional honor.

And he talks of my responsibilities, she thought, when he's central to so many people's lives—the chief man of this island, quite apart from his business ventures.

He wasn't awkward with the baby, she saw. He handled the small bundle with complete assurance, instantly soothing an experimental wail of protest, lifting the baby to a more comfortable position against his shoulder, his smile softening to tenderness as the tiny angry face relaxed back into slumber.

She thought, with a pang, He should have children of his own, then paused, her throat constricting in self-derision. He was playing the part expected of him, that was all.

Nic Xandreou had already tried the obligations of marriage, and found them not to his taste, she reminded herself with an effort. His life belonged now in boardrooms and penthouses, and wherever else there was money to be made and pleasure to be enjoyed.

She glanced back, and found him looking at her, one eyebrow raised interrogatively. He said laconically, 'Hara wants you to hold him now.'

'Oh, no.' Camilla took an alarmed step backwards. 'I'd really rather not. I might drop him. I'm not used to small babies.'

'Then start accustoming yourself.' His quiet voice brooked no opposition. 'Sit on the bed, if you feel safer that way. You cannot hurt Hara by refusing.'

He pushed her down gently on to the edge of the mattress, and put the baby into her reluctant arms amid another chorus of approval.

She looked down at the shawl-swathed cocoon. One small starfish hand had emerged from the wrappings, and moved to splay against her breast. A tiny bubble escaped the pursed lips as the baby's head turned—seeking.

Strange anguish lanced through her as she wondered for the first time in her life what it would be like to bear a child to the man you loved. To be the focus, as Hara was, of his pride and adoration.

She thought, I wish—oh, God, I wish... and stopped dead, transfixed by the realisation of precisely what she wished.

As if magnetised, she looked up at Nic, her eyes widening, her parted lips tremulous. His face was sombre and aloof, a muscle working beside his mouth as if he was trying to control some angry emotion.

He probably resented the way she, a stranger, and an unwanted outsider at that, had been drawn into this intimate family moment, she thought painfully. Nor could she blame him, considering the deception she was practising on him.

He said softly, 'You are supposed to say something.'

She bit her lip, and turned to Hara. 'The baby's very handsome,' she said. 'Like his father.'

Judging by Hara's delighted beam as Nic translated, and the shout of laughter and acclaim from the others, she'd managed to find the right comment, outsider or not.

Hara bent forward, speaking rapidly in Greek, and Camilla shook her head in incomprehension.

Dimitris supplied the cheerful explanation.
'My wife hopes that Xandreou's woman also
bears many fine sons.'

Camilla felt a wave of helpless colour sweep
up into her face. She did not dare look at Nic
as he bent and took the baby from her, re-
storing him to his mother. But, to her relief,
the room began to empty, and they were conducted outside where tables had been set with
platters of bread, salad and sliced fruit, and
jugs of red wine.

Nic was escorted ceremoniously to the place
of honour, but Camilla was surrounded by the
women, and pulled away to another table where
she was subjected to a friendly but thorough
scrutiny, everything from the colour of her hair
to the material of her dress being examined and
exclaimed over.

Her throat taut with embarrassment, Camilla
managed to smile as she swallowed some
grapes, and drank a glass of the wine, aware
that Nic was watching ironically.

But she had only herself to blame, she
thought. If she hadn't gone along with
Arianna's suggestion and pushed herself on to
him for the day, she'd have been saved all this
discomfiture. She could only pray that back at
the Villa Apollo everything had worked out,
and that the end would, somehow, justify the
means she'd chosen.

The celebration seemed endless, although she
supposed she should be grateful for that. The
longer it extended into the afternoon, the less

time she would have to spend on her own with him, and the less opportunity there would be for the kind of self-betrayal she dreaded, she thought constrictedly.

She was conscious of him all the time. Above the laughter and chatter of the women there seemed to be a silent zone where the two of them existed alone. A place where she could look at him, and smile, and say the words of love and desire she dared not even think. Where his kisses burned on her parted lips, and her body bloomed under the touch of his hands. A secret place, she thought, which would haunt her for the rest of her life, tormenting her with all kinds of unfulfilled yearnings.

When she felt his hand curve round her shoulder in reality, she almost cried out in longing, but when she looked up at him his face was remote, his eyes guarded.

'It is time we went.' His tone was crisp, formal. 'Please say your goodbyes.'

Mechanically, Camilla began to assemble her few Greek phrases of thanks and farewell.

A stranger, she thought, not a lover. That was what he was, and that was how he must remain for her sanity's sake.

They were escorted back to the harbour, and helped enthusiastically on board *Calliope*. As they headed out of the bay, Camilla waved until the figures on the quay became mere dots.

'You enjoyed that?' Nic asked quietly from the tiller.

'Of course,' Camilla said with slight constraint. 'I felt very—privileged to be made so welcome.'

He was silent for a moment. 'They are simple people,' he said at last. 'I hope their—lack of inhibition didn't distress you.'

'No.' Her face warmed again. 'I suppose they were bound to draw the obvious conclusion.' She tried to laugh. 'Everyone else has.'

'Yes.' The monosyllable was clipped and curt, and she ventured no other comment.

The breeze had dropped, and the afternoon was still, the horizon a shimmer of heat. Camilla felt a trickle of sweat run down between her breasts. She put her hands to the nape of her neck, lifting away the heavy fall of hair.

It occurred to her suddenly that Nic had not turned *Calliope* back the way they'd come, but that they were sailing on round the island.

She looked at him. 'Where are we going?'

'I know a small bay where the swimming is good,' he returned. 'I thought we could anchor there for a while.' He paused again. 'And also—talk.' He slanted a smile at her, his eyes flicking over her breasts, and down to where the thin cotton dress clung to the line of her thigh.

'About what?' Camilla hunched a defensive shoulder, aware that her pulses had begun to thump erratically.

'We have negotiations to conduct,' he reminded her silkily. 'Or had you forgotten?'

'By no means,' she retorted. 'But I thought this was the time of day when all business stopped.'

His smile widened. 'That, *agape mou*, rather depends on the nature of the business—and its urgency.' He left the words tingling between them, and turned *Calliope* towards the shore again.

Camilla found herself staring blankly at the small horseshoe of pale sand sheltered by two stony outcrops that they were approaching. From the beach, the ground rose into a wilderness of bleached rock smudged by the occasional olive tree. It was very quiet—very lonely.

She swallowed. Keep him talking, she thought, touching her dry lips with the tip of her tongue. Make it formal—a discussion of terms. The problem was she hadn't had time to do her homework—to find out the kind of hypothetical sum she'd be expected to ask for on Katie's behalf. She had no real idea what bargaining power she could command.

But Nic Xandreou knew, down to the last drachma, and could call her bluff whenever he chose.

But what else did he know—or suspect? That was the real risk—the danger she needed to be on her guard against.

'*Matia mou*,' he had called her. And she must never let him look into her eyes again in case he saw the pitiful truth she needed at all cost to conceal: that, against all logic, reason or even sanity, she was in love with him.

CHAPTER TEN

NIC dropped anchor some hundred and fifty yards from the shore. With the noise of the engine stilled, there was only the creak of *Calliope*'s timbers and the soft lap of the sea to break the hot and heavy afternoon silence. To remind Camilla, if any reminder were needed, just how alone they were. Shading her eyes with her hand, she stared towards the beach as if mesmerised by it.

'Can you swim so far?' He was standing just behind her. He spoke softly, his breath fanning her ear.

'Of course.' She kept her tone brisk and bright. 'I'm not that much of a wimp.'

'No,' he said rather drily. 'That much is certain. But, all the same, we will take the boat ashore.'

Camilla watched as he brought the small dinghy alongside, loading it with towels, straw mats, a basket containing food and wine, and even a sun umbrella brought up from *Calliope*'s cabin.

All the gear for a successful seduction conveniently to hand, she thought, swallowing. But then she'd hardly be the first girl he'd have brought to this remote and lovely place.

She trailed her hand in the water as they rowed ashore. Shoals of small fish darted here and there, and soft fronds of weed billowed and danced in the shadowy depths.

Her feet sank into the hot sand as she helped him drag the boat up the beach. By the time they'd unloaded it, Camilla felt that her dress was sticking to her. Surreptitiously, she eased the cling of the fabric away from her thighs.

But he'd noticed, of course.

'Shall we cool off before we open our discussions?' Nic wedged the sun umbrella in place with a couple of large stones, and dusted off his hands. Camilla watched with misgiving as he unfastened the remaining buttons on his shirt. She was suddenly, forcibly reminded of the first time she'd seen him. Did he usually swim naked? she wondered, dry-mouthed. And, if so, would this occasion be any exception?

But to her relief he stripped off his shorts to reveal brief black trunks. He turned, encountering her scrutiny with a mockingly lifted eyebrow. The faint smile playing round his mouth was a challenge as he waited for her to fumble clumsily out of her dress, and drop it with self-conscious awkwardness on to one of the straw mats.

'Your scratches are healed now?' He took her arm, turning her slightly so that he could study the fading marks.

Flushing, Camilla pulled free. 'Completely.' She kicked off her sandals and ran past him down to the edge of the sea.

The water felt breath-stoppingly cool against her over-heated skin as she splashed through the shallows.

'Have a care.' Nic was beside her, overtaking her with ease. 'The beach shelves quickly and very steeply. You can soon find you are out of your depth.'

I found that out a long time ago. She thought it, but did not say it, as she watched him take a running dive, the lean, dark body cutting the water with hardly a splash.

She'd been out of her depth since the moment she arrived on Karthos. She'd been so sure of her ability to handle things, but looking back it seemed she might just have made the situation worse. Lending herself to this deception seemed the only way to make amends to Katie, but she had also to gauge the consequences to herself. Physical damage healed. Emotional scarring could be with you for life.

Other girls at the secretarial agency came back from foreign holidays giggling over brief flings with waiters, couriers or ski instructors, but for Camilla there could be no guilty secrets to be shared with a smile and sigh over coffee.

Because Nic Xandreou mattered, she thought as she slid down into the water, letting it take and lift her, closing her eyes against the dazzle of the sunlight. He was in her mind and her heart, part of the fibre of her being, and she

hadn't the least idea how or when it had begun
to happen. She'd been in too deep before she'd
even seen the danger.

But what she needed to remember, above all,
was that it wasn't mutual. She was an annoyance to Nic—a small problem to be resolved, and that was all. If he made love to her,
it would be with cynical amusement at the ease
with which his victory had been accomplished.
A trifling bonus on another successful deal.

And the knowledge of that more than out-
weighed the transitory delight of being, for a
few hours, Xandreou's woman. It had to.

She turned to glance at the shore, and saw
with a shock of alarm that she'd let herself drift
further out than she'd intended. She was a
competent enough swimmer, but she was accustomed to the predictability of swimming-
baths. Beneath her now were untold fathoms
of the Ionian Sea. She trod water, breathing
deeply and calmly, refusing to panic as she felt
the pull of an unsuspected current.

She glanced around, but could see no reassuring dark head within hailing distance.
Besides, she didn't want to call for help unnecessarily, especially when she'd been quite
implicitly warned.

The boat, she realised, biting her lip, seemed
marginally nearer than the beach. She would
swim there first—make some excuse about
preferring to sunbathe on board, which was
probably a safer option anyway.

She was halfway there when she realised she was in difficulty. The current seemed stronger, constantly hampering her progress, and her arms and legs were getting heavy.

She thought, This is stupid, and a small wave broke against her face, making her cough, increasing the frightened tightness in her chest.

One answer was to turn on to her back again and float, but that would leave her at the mercy of the current, and it seemed best to flounder on, fighting panic and fatigue.

She'd told him her swimming was 'good enough' but it seemed she'd overestimated her capabilities.

She opened her mouth to shout, swallowed more water, and almost submerged, choking. Through streaming eyes, she saw that *Calliope* looked further away than ever.

Suddenly there was a dark shape beside her in the water, the sea churned, and Nic was there, shaking the water out of his eyes, his face dark with anger. She heard him say something in furious Greek, then his arms went round her, lifting her up, holding her against him.

'Relax, little fool,' his voice bit at her. 'I have you now.'

He turned her effortlessly, supporting her as he used a smooth, powerful side-stroke to take them back to shore.

'It is safe now.' His voice was terse as his clasp slackened. He lowered her gently, and

Camilla discovered sand and shingle under her feet, her legs buckling in sheer relief.

Nic muttered something under his breath, then his arms were round her again, and he was carrying her up the beach.

Camilla found herself deposited under the shade of the umbrella. She looked up at him. He was dark against the sun, sea-water droplets glistening on his tanned body. Her chest hurt, and she could taste nothing but salt, but all the same she felt a twist of hot, shamed excitement deep within her. She said hoarsely, 'I'm sorry.'

'I did warn you.' His shrug was almost impatient. 'But there was no real danger. Lie quietly for a while.'

Through half-closed eyes, she watched him busy himself with the food basket. Heard the subdued pop of a wine cork being withdrawn.

'Drink this.' The glass he gave her was crystal with a twisted stem. Just the thing for a beach picnic, the fragment of her mind still working normally noted drily.

Her teeth chattered against the rim of the glass. His hand came up to steady it, and the brush of his fingers against hers made her shiver.

The wine was cold, crisp and dry, but it brought warmth to the frozen, frightened place inside her, and steadied the uneven rush of her pulses.

When she had finished, he silently took the glass from her hand, and replaced it with a fresh bread roll crammed with cold roast lamb.

She began, 'Oh, I don't think...' but he silenced her with a lifted hand.

'It is little wonder you tired so easily,' he told her curtly. 'At Dimitris's house, of course, you only pretended to eat.'

'I wasn't—I'm not hungry,' she protested without conviction. Actually she was ravenous. Maybe frightening yourself silly had that effect. But she doubted whether she could swallow a morsel.

She was too aware of him, of his proximity, the sheen of his bronze skin, the damp tendrils of hair curling on his forehead and at the nape of his neck, and above all his own unique male scent commingling with the tang of salt. Although he was no longer touching her, she felt as if she was being tied in knots. Fool, she castigated herself inwardly.

'I don't save a woman from drowning merely to watch her starve in front of me.' He was implacable.

Mutely, she bit into the roll, the slices of lamb were thick and juicy, enhanced by a sprinkling of salt, and there were big, firm-fleshed tomatoes as an accompaniment, with sharp black olives, and more of the wine. It was one of the simplest meals she'd ever eaten, and she would remember it, she thought, for the whole of her life.

She wiped her hands on a paper napkin. 'Thank you,' she said stiltedly.

'The thanks are due to Hara's mother,' he said with a shrug. 'She packed the basket and put it on the boat for me.' He slanted a smile at her. 'She says you are too thin. That I should look after you better.' He paused. 'God knows what she would say about the events of the past half-hour.'

Camilla sat up straight. 'Nothing, I hope. I'm grateful for what you did, of course.' She steadied her voice. 'But it's not your business to look after me at all, and you should have told her so.'

'No,' he said. 'Because she would not understand. In her world, a woman belongs to a man. Her father first, then her husband.'

'How cosy.' Camilla lifted her chin. 'The twentieth century has clearly passed Karthos by.'

'Not all of it.' His voice was cool, and the firm mouth seemed to tighten in momentary bitterness.

She knew he was thinking of his wife. There were a hundred questions teeming in her brain, but she resisted them, lying back on her straw mat, and pretending to close her eyes.

'Don't fall asleep in the sun,' he advised drily. 'Or you could have third-degree burns to add to your other problems.'

Camilla grimaced swiftly, then rummaged for the protective lotion she used. She said lightly. 'I seem to be a walking disaster today.'

'Not just today.' The contradiction was flat, with an underlying note of anger. 'You have caused difficulties ever since you arrived here.'

'You're not so easy to deal with yourself.' Camilla began to apply the lotion to her arms and legs, glad to bend her head and let her damp hair form a curtain against the brooding intensity of his gaze.

'I did not intend to be,' he reminded her. 'Yet here we are.' He paused. 'Shall negotiations begin?'

'Yes.' She was smoothing the lotion over the swell of her breasts above the brief bikini cups, and across the flatness of her abdomen, acutely aware that he was following every movement, a faint smile curling the corners of his mouth. There was reminiscence in that smile, and something altogether more edged and dangerous that she preferred not to analyse. 'At least, I—I suppose so.'

The smile widened. He held out his hand. 'Turn over, *matia mou*, and I will oil your back.'

'No, thank you, Kyrios Nicos.' She replaced the cap on the bottle very precisely. The last thing in the world she could afford was to feel his hands on her again, she thought, a sharp tremor running through her senses. 'As you've reminded me, I'm not here to sunbathe.'

'Such formality,' he mocked.

'A business meeting is a formal occasion.' She gave him a direct look. 'Although today you've let me see how kind you can be—to all sorts of people. I only wish you could spare some kindness for Katie, and Spiro.'

He shrugged. 'Sometimes the greatest kindness lies in cruelty. I'm sure you've heard that.'

'Yes,' she said. 'But I'm not sure I believe it.'

'Then you should,' he said softly. 'Also that you should not let your heart rule your head. That can lead only to—disaster.'

Camilla looked up at the fierce blue arc of the sky. She heard herself say, 'Was it here that you met her—your wife?' and braced herself for an icy snub, or, at worst, an explosion.

'Yes, it was here.' He looked away at the horizon. 'They used the north of the island as location for a film—a thriller.' His smile was wintry. 'Not a very good one. It never went on general release. And she was afraid, I think, that her career would never amount to more than films like that.' He shrugged slightly. 'She was ready for a change of direction—which I provided.'

Camilla's breath caught in her throat. She said, 'There must have been more to it than that.'

'Oh, at first, yes. There was certainly passion.' His voice slowed to a drawl. 'She was a beautiful, radiant creature, my Rachelle. To make love with her was to taste paradise. Every day was filled with sunshine. It was easy to forget that winter must follow.'

He looked down at the glass he held, twisting its stem in his lean, strong fingers. Hands that could crush, if they chose, Camilla thought, as well as rescue—and caress. His words were like bruises on her mind. 'A beautiful, radiant creature'. Quite the opposite to ordinary Camilla Dryden.

To her surprise, his voice went on. 'At first, she loved it here.' His tone was quiet, almost reflective. 'She thought it quaint. That should have warned me. It was the view of a tourist— someone passing through, who looks but does not see. She knew that I had other homes in other places, but this was my island—the place to which I would always return. She seemed to accept that. She seemed also to want, as I did, a settled life—children.'

His mouth twisted. 'I forgot, of course, that she was an actress. For a while it suited her to play the part of my wife—docile and devoted. Then she began to want more—always more. Whenever I went away, she insisted on going too, even though I'd warned her it would not always be possible—that there were times when I had to travel light and fast. Rachelle needed her entourage—her maid, a major domo to ensure fresh flowers and champagne in every suite, her personal chef. She needed to be centre-stage, but with me there were times when work had to come first, when I could not be there at the restaurants—the theatres— the parties.'

His voice was weary. 'She was like a child robbed of its toys. She was lonely—I neglected her. She was young and she would enjoy herself—with me or without me——'

'Please,' Camilla broke in urgently. 'You don't have to tell me this.'

'Ah, but I do.' For a moment the dark eyes glittered at her. His voice deepened. 'You asked the question; you must listen to the answer—all of it, if you wish to understand.' He looked away again, his brows drawing together as if he was in pain. 'It was at one of those parties I could not attend that Rachelle began to experiment seriously with the drug that eventually killed her.'

He sighed. 'I knew there had been earlier experiences, but she'd sworn her involvement had been minimal—that it was behind her. I was caught up in a deal, working day and night. I—missed the warning signs.' He tossed back the remains of his wine, and replaced the glass in the basket.

'Perhaps I didn't want to see them. When I realised what was going on, I arranged for her to have treatment. She wept, clung to me, swore it would never happen again. She was just so bored . . .'

He flung his head back, the muscles in his throat taut. 'I wanted so badly to believe her. I blamed myself for leaving her so much to herself. I had realised, of course, by then that our expectations of marriage were completely opposed. But I still thought a child might heal the breach—give some purpose to our lives.'

He paused. 'Then she told me her former agent had been in touch—that she had the chance of a major role.' His voice was hard as stone, and Camilla felt her heart twist in pity at the starkness in his face. 'I had my life, she said; she should be allowed to have hers. There would be plenty of time in the future for children, if we still wanted them. In the meantime, she had been advised to play down her marriage altogether.'

He laughed bitterly. 'She could have said nothing more damaging to my pride—to my sense of family. I was angry. We quarrelled, and I left. I think I expected her to follow. But she did not. For a while she had all the success she had dreamed of. But it was never enough. She always wanted a new sensation—a new high—and there was one sure way to provide it.

'She continued to be treated for addiction. Although we were apart, almost completely estranged, I paid at first. Later it was the studio, until she became totally unreliable and they sacked her.'

He cleared his throat. 'She called me—told me she was going underground—renting a cabin in the hills while she tried to get her head together. That she needed to be alone.' He made a small sound in his throat. 'She was found in the motel room a week later. She had not been there alone—far from it—but none of her—companions ever came forward.'

'Oh, God.' Camilla forced the words from a dry throat.

He turned his head slowly and looked at her. 'You wonder why I have told you this—spoken of things I hoped were buried forever? It is to make you understand at last why I must protect my family—stop them from making the same mistakes as I did.' His shrug was cynical. 'Oh, you will tell me that Catherine is not Rachelle. That my wife carried within her the seeds of her own destruction. But it is not that simple.'

He beat a clenched fist into the palm of his hand. 'When you are young, you think love can solve everything—that it can tear down the barriers of background and culture. Overcome all difficulties and misunderstandings.' He shook his head. 'I know that is a fallacy. I had money, and power, but I could not offer Rachelle what she wanted, or save her from what she ultimately chose.

'And I will not have Spiro hurt as I was—constantly reaching for your sister across a widening abyss of bitterness and estrangement.'

It was all there in his voice—the anger, the regret, the underlying sense of desolation.

There was a loneliness, an isolation in the tense, dark figure beside her that caught Camilla by the throat. Although the things he'd spoken of were light-years from her own experience, the instinct to offer some kind of comfort, however inadequate, was overwhelming.

Kneeling beside him, she said his name. Put a hand tentatively on the smooth skin of his shoulder. Felt the hard muscle clench beneath her touch, and the harsh tremor which seemed to shake his whole body.

He turned to her swiftly, almost savagely, a dark flame in his eyes and burning on his mouth as it possessed hers. Camilla kissed him back, her lips parting to allow the urgent, aching dart of his tongue, her first shy response becoming ardent as the shackles of restraint fell away. Nic's arms went round her hard, tightening almost convulsively as if he was trying to fuse their bodies into a single entity, as the kiss went on, blurring reality into a fevered awareness only of themselves, and a need that could not be denied.

Camilla was breathing his breath, absorbed into the fierce hurry of his heartbeat. When his weight carried her backwards, downwards on to the straw mat, she had no thought of resistance. Her hands went up to hold him—to claim him as her man. To offer herself as his woman.

For a moment, he reared above her, his breathing ragged, his eyes searching her face. Then he said hoarsely, '*Matia mou*,' and bent to her.

Impatiently, he wrenched the fragile bikini-top apart, then cupped her bare breasts in his hands, lifting them so that his lips could explore their delicate roundness more fully. She felt her nipples harden in sensuous response, the joy of this remembered intimacy invading her like a warm tide. His mouth closed over one rosy tumescent peak, tugging persuasively at first, then more compellingly, forcing a husky moan of pleasure from her taut throat.

He laughed softly against her skin. 'Is that good, *pedhi mou*—my little one?'

Her voice cracked. 'Oh, God, you must know...'

'Yes,' he said on a breath of satisfaction. 'Now I know.' He began to kiss her again, his mouth feathering against hers, demanding, yet withholding, in a teasing but wholly inexorable arousal.

'Touch me, *agape mou*,' he whispered hoarsely. 'I need to feel your hands on me.'

She reached for him, hands framing his face, feeling the faint roughness along his jawline, then clung to his shoulders, her body arching like a cat's as his own fingers moved slowly down her body in soft, stroking exploration, tracing the gentle valley between her breasts, the fragile shell of her ribcage, the tender flesh inside her elbows, and down to the pulses fluttering like humming birds in her wrists, and across to the flat plane of her stomach, and the delicate thrust of her hipbones.

Where his hands moved, his mouth followed like sweet, dangerous fire, tasting her as if she were some exquisite banquet arrayed for his delectation.

Camilla moved restlessly, little helpless sounds breaking from her throat, as she strayed down her own tactile paths, her hands gliding over the strength of bone and fierce tension of muscle. There was a warmth inside her as potent as the great brazen sun above them, and an ache as deep as the restless sea. For the first time in her life, she was totally at the mercy of needs she had never imagined. The carefully structured barriers of control and reserve had splintered into sensation now, and yearning.

She was hardly aware that the caressing hands had stripped away her bikini briefs, until he touched her at the silken, molten core of her womanhood, the lean fingers stroking her, lifting her on to a dizzying spiral of blind, moaning acceptance.

Through half-closed eyes she saw him rear over her, head and shoulders gilded by an aura like flame. He was naked too now, a god of bronze and copper.

Apollo, she thought dazedly, whose sun was around her, and within her, devouring her—consuming her.

She felt the sleek velvet hardness of him between her thighs, seeking her. His hands were beneath her, raising her—challenging her to meet his urgency with her own.

For a moment, the tautness of her inner muscles resisted his penetration, and a small shocked sob rose in her throat. Nic bent his head, his mouth closing on hers, stifling the tiny sound, whispering soft words of reassurance, as, slowly and with forbearance, he coaxed her body to relax again, and yield up its last secret to him.

Sheathed within her, he held her close for a while, his lips soothing her with gentle sensuality, as she accustomed herself to the reality of this, the ultimate intimacy.

Then, still without haste, he began to move, smoothly, easily, luring her to join him, to echo the eternal rhythms of passion, so strange to her, and yet, at the same time, so right and familiar.

Pleasure began slowly to unfurl inside her like a leaf in spring, beckoning her to a deeper response. She clung to him, fingers digging into his sweat-slicked shoulders, legs locked round his waist, letting her body pulse in time with his, the sudden harshness of her breathing echoing, commingling with Nic's. All her being, mental and physical, was concentrated now—fixed, almost with bewilderment, on the flowering of these new, intense sensations deep within her.

With every powerful thrust of Nic's loins, she seemed to be carried nearer some nameless but attainable goal, driven on by instinct, seeking blindly for some surcease from the fierce maelstrom of craving he'd created in her.

Every nerve-ending was vibrating suddenly. She was gasping for breath, her head thrashing wildly from side to side, her mouth framing words of need—of entreaty.

'Yes.' His voice seemed to reach her from some vast distance. 'Yes, *agape mou*.'

She felt a faint judder, down in the depths of her being, a sweet, hot, ineffable trembling that was spreading, gaining momentum, taking possession of her, forcing her into an upward spiral of sharp, half-crazy delight.

She could hear herself moaning, her voice thick, like a stranger's, as the spiral deepened, intensified almost unbearably, keeping her on the screaming edge of some undreamed-of sensation.

Then, as she thought she could stand no more—that she was going to die—the spiral broke, and she was free, her body convulsed by tremors as strong as the earth, her mind torn apart by the exquisite savagery of her release.

As she fought for breath, for sanity, she heard Nic's breathing change, quicken hoarsely. She saw him fling back his head suddenly, the muscles in his throat like whipcord, his face strained, almost anguished. Then she felt, like silken fire, the molten reality of his own climax.

She held him close, floating down with him from one plane of golden, honeyed satisfaction to the next, as their bodies quietened and gave them peace at last.

CHAPTER ELEVEN

I LOVE you.

Camilla pressed her mouth to the damp, heated skin of Nic's shoulder, damming back the words which rang in her head, and sang in her heart. Words, she reminded herself, that he would not want to hear from her—ever.

The realisation chilled through the heavenly euphoria which had succeeded their love-making. Up to then, she'd been lying in his arms, head pillowed on his chest, enjoying the touch of his fingers as they lazily caressed the curve of her hip.

Now, she moved restively as awareness flooded back, alerting other emotions. Reminding her with merciless clarity precisely how far she'd allowed herself to stray from her self-imposed guidelines of morality and common sense.

She sat up abruptly, reaching for her bikini with hands that shook.

'What is it?' Nic lifted himself on to an elbow and studied her, a faint frown drawing the dark brows together.

'Nothing,' she said, then amended swiftly, 'Just that it's getting late, that's all.'

'Is that really all, *matia mou*?' He took her chin in his hand, forcing her to meet his gaze. 'I think I see regret in your eyes.'

'Well, please don't worry about it.' Her voice was brittle as she jerked herself away from his grasp. 'I can't imagine I'm the first to be swept away by your fabulous technique, and come to her senses when it's too late.'

His gaze sharpened. 'You think I planned this? Let me remind you that you asked to come with me today.'

'I haven't forgotten.' Her laugh cracked in the middle. ' "Those whom the gods wish to destroy, they first make mad." I should have remembered that.'

'Madness?' Nic shook his head. 'I think it was the hand of fate which brought us together here.'

'I don't believe in fate.' She'd said that before—a lifetime ago. Now fate had punished her lack of faith with the cruellest of revenges. She lifted her chin. 'You said you could have me whenever you wanted. It must be wonderful to be infallible.'

'Don't talk like a fool,' he said with sudden brusqueness. 'You must believe me, Camilla. I did not intend this to happen.'

'Oh, I do believe it.' Fighting for control, she laced her tone with scorn. 'Two paternity suits in one family might be too much to handle, even for you.'

'Is that all that concerns you?' His voice was very quiet. 'The legal—financial implications?'

'What else is there?' She felt very weary suddenly, and close to tears. 'That's what we came here to discuss in the first place.' She buried her teeth in her lower lip. 'Until, of course, I let myself be so expertly side-tracked.'

Nic reached for his own clothes, began to drag them on. 'Then perhaps all future discussions should be conducted by our lawyers,' he said harshly. 'Then there will be no danger of any—personal element intruding.'

'Our lawyers'. Camilla found herself thinking numbly of elderly Mr Cranshaw who had dealt so kindly with the aftermath of her parents' death. Was he up to the kind of hard-nosed legal battle which the Xandreou legal experts could enforce? Somehow she didn't think so.

Because she didn't yet know, of course, what had transpired at the Villa Apollo in their absence. They were all taking it for granted that if Spiro regained his memory he would still want Katie and acknowledge his baby. But nothing was certain in this hideously shifting world. Maybe Nic's undoubted influence over his brother would prevail in the end after all. Spiro might well decide he could not afford to disregard his brother's plans for his future.

I came here to help, she thought. And all I've managed to do is make everything a thousand times worse—not just for Katie, but for myself as well.

The possibility of a future as a single mother was just too hideous to contemplate. But it was what she'd invited just the same.

Just the touch of Nic's mouth on hers, the brush of his fingers on her skin, and all her resolve seemed to melt away in a need that transcended common sense and logic. And she would have to live with the consequences, whatever they were.

Her life was in pieces, at any rate, she acknowledged with a kind of desperate clarity. Somehow she had to drag it into shape again. Dismiss this pitiful creature at the mercy of her own physicality. Find again the cool, sensible persona she'd once possessed.

If I can, she thought sorrowfully. If that girl still exists. Or is she now, no more, no less, for better or worse, simply Xandreou's woman?

The return trip was a silent one. Camilla sat in the bow, staring ahead of her. The sea had darkened into a faint swell, and the air seemed still and almost threatening—or was that merely the suggestion of her own inner tensions?

She'd presumed that Nic would return her to the beach below the sea house, but instead he turned *Calliope* towards the landing stage below the Villa Apollo. She turned questioningly, and saw him laying aside a pair of binoculars, his black brows drawn together in a frown.

A tremor of apprehension crept down her spine. Peering ahead, she could just make out a figure on the landing stage, his arms sema-phoring for attention.

Yannis, she thought, swallowing. And no prizes for guessing the reason behind the frantic signals either. She straightened her shoulders, bracing herself mentally. Nic was angry enough as it was. When he found out he'd been duped . . .

Her heart was hammering. She found herself wordlessly begging Apollo the Healer to make it somehow all right.

They arrived at the landing stage, Nic throwing Yannis a rope as the other man burst into a flood of excited Greek. Nic listened tautly, his mouth set in grim lines. When Yannis paused for breath, he nodded curtly, then turned and looked at Camilla, the dark eyes narrowed, his face harsh with silent accu-sation. Helplessly, she gazed back at him, trying not to let him see that she was shaking.

He swung himself lithely on to the landing stage, and he and Yannis began to run up the sloping narrow path which led to the villa. Camilla had no choice but to follow. The leaves and twigs of unknown shrubs brushed her as she passed. Something with thorns caught her dress and she tore it free as she ran. In the dis-tance, she heard the first faint rumble of thunder.

A storm, she thought, a bubble of hysteria welling up inside her. There was going to be a storm, and she needed to reach the villa before it broke. The path became steps, and she went up them, two at a time, breathless but driving herself on. There was a glimmer of turquoise ahead of her somewhere that she knew was the swimming-pool, and she pushed through the last of the encircling bushes, throat dry, heart hammering, hand pressed to the stitch in her side.

The little tableau had been established on the terrace outside the *saloni*.

Spiro was in a chair, his injured leg supported by a stool. Katie stood beside him, her hand in his. It was as simple as that, but their tranquillity, their happiness, their sense of total belonging was almost tangible.

Camilla halted, her throat tightening, tears stinging at her eyes. They looked so right together, she thought. Surely Nic would be able to see that, and forgive.

But he didn't look particularly compassionate, she saw with a pang. He was quietly, furiously angry, colour burning along his cheekbones, his mouth a straight line.

He was a powerful man. His rage could be destructive, and Spiro and Katie were so young, so vulnerable. She wanted to get between them, to use herself as a shield.

He said softly in English, 'So, little brother, your memory has returned. God be thanked.'

'Yes.' Spiro spoke in the same language. 'And, with Providence, you must also thank Katie, who is soon to be my wife.' The words were calm, measured. He lifted Katie's hand and pressed it to his cheek in a gesture of tender possession, then gave Nic a level look. 'I hope, Nicos, our marriage will have your blessing, but I must warn you it will happen anyway, whatever you decide.'

'Then you have not recovered your senses along with your memory. A pity.' Nic's voice was harsh.

'Nic.' Arianna, who had been standing in the shadow by the long windows with Dr Deroulades, and an anxious Eleni, interposed herself. 'Katie has given Spiro back to us—like a miracle. You must accept their love, approve it—welcome Katie to our family.'

'Be silent.' He didn't even look at her. 'Go to your room, Arianna. I shall not forget your part in this. Or yours, Petros,' he added as Arianna, unwontedly subdued, turned away into the house, her fist pressed to her mouth.

The doctor said quietly, 'That was a risk I had to take for Spiro's sake. I must always think it was worth it. And now your brother should rest.'

Nic's body was taut as a bowstring. 'Of course.' He looked at Katie. 'Yannis will drive you back to the sea house, *thespinis*. You—and your sister.'

'No.' Spiro shook his head, his tone suddenly fierce. 'Katie stays here. My mistake was ever to allow her out of my sight.'

'And my error was to allow you out of mine.' The retort was hard, but Nic walked over to the chair, bending to draw his brother into a fierce embrace. For a long moment they held each other in silence.

Camilla found herself choking back a sob. Over the sea a streak of fire forked through the darkening sky, to be followed almost at once by an ominous growl.

She watched Spiro helped up on to his crutches, Katie assisting, her young face furrowed in concern, as the small procession wended its way into the villa.

Leaving her alone with Nic in the gathering storm.

'Quite a conspiracy.' His tone was deceptively laconic. The hooded eyes told her nothing. 'Was anyone not involved, I wonder, apart from Yannis and Eleni?'

She touched her tongue to her dry lips. 'I— I didn't want to deceive you, but there seemed no other way to give Katie and Spiro their chance.'

'And I played right into your beguiling hands,' he said softly, his mouth curling in contempt. 'My congratulations. You were most—convincing in your efforts to hold my attention—even to making the ultimate sacrifice.' He shook his head in cynical wonderment. 'Can sisterly devotion ever ask more?'

His voice cut her like a whip. She flinched and stepped back.

'It wasn't like that. You know that.'

'No?' His brows lifted. 'Then tell me how it was, honey girl, with your saint's eyes and sinner's body.'

I loved you, she thought. I wanted to make up to you for all the pain—all the loneliness. And now I've brought it all down on myself instead, because I can't tell you.

'Well?' he said too gently. 'I am waiting.'

Camilla bit her lip. 'You talk as if I planned it somehow...' She stopped abruptly, colour rushing into her face as she realised he was laughing soundlessly.

'No, no, *agape mou*. You forget. That was what you accused *me* of doing. Quite a masterstroke, all that injured, ruined innocence. The seducer reproached by his victim.' His voice deepened in harsh mockery. 'A second accomplished actress to add to my collection, and I never guessed.'

Another lightning flash flickered in the sky, the accompanying thunder closer, louder.

'I wondered what you were hiding from me, *matia mou*,' the relentless voice went on. 'And now I know—the corruption behind the mask of virtue. The lies behind the appearance of candour. No wonder you didn't want me to look into your eyes.'

The sky was pressing down on her. The air felt thick, making it difficult to breathe.

She saw that Yannis had returned, and was waiting, hands on hips, for Nic's orders. Orders that would take her back to the sea house and away from him forever.

Here, she thought unsteadily, here, where it had begun, was where it would end in acrimony, bitterness and misunderstanding. The wheel had come full circle.

She said huskily, 'You must believe what you want. I thought I was acting for the best. And please don't punish Katie for my mistakes. Just remember—she reached for Spiro across the abyss—and brought him to safety.'

She turned and walked away, moving almost blindly, as the first heavy drops of rain began to fall.

Camilla folded a white cotton shirt and laid it on top of her case then glanced round the room, checking the empty cupboards and drawers. But no trace of her brief occupation remained.

It was very quiet in the sea house. Soula had gone to visit her sister in a neighbouring village, and Yannis was driving Katie and Spiro into the mountains for dinner at a romantically remote taverna.

'Come with us,' Katie had urged. 'Darling, you can't spend your last evening on your own.'

'Oh, but I can.' Camilla had smiled at her. 'I've no intention, my pet, of playing gooseberry. Anyway, I've far too much to do this evening. I'm catching the early ferry, remember.'

In spite of Katie's protests, Camilla had insisted on returning to England before the wedding.

'I can't try Mrs Strathmore's patience any further,' she'd said. 'I need that job. And anyway, now that Spiro's hopping around on crutches, you'll be off to the mainland to meet the rest of the Xandreou clan.'

'Yes.' Katie had grimaced slightly. 'The aunts in the Peloponnese sound a bit formidable.'

'You'll have them eating out of your hand in no time,' Camilla had reassured her. 'Then, before you know it, you'll be married.'

But for all her brave words, the last thing in the world she'd wanted was her own company tonight. But making a third with Katie and Spiro, being on the edge of their coruscating happiness, was more than she could handle, she thought wretchedly.

It had undoubtedly been the worst week of her life.

She'd returned to the sea house on the night of the storm, wandering through the rooms, unable to sleep, or even relax, while it raged itself out.

She'd been hollow-eyed and on edge, in contrast to the calm serenity of the following morning, hoping and praying for some message from Nic. But there had been nothing.

The things he'd said, the way he'd looked at her with such contempt, seemed to be seared across her consciousness.

It had been almost a relief to hear from Arianna that he'd gone to Athens.

'And I hope his Zoe puts him in a better temper,' she'd added sourly. 'He is still barely speaking to me. Of course he is pleased about Spiro, but he cannot bear to be wrong.'

'I shouldn't imagine it happens very often,' Camilla had said drily, biting her lip until she tasted blood as an image of Nic, naked with a sinuous Greek beauty in his arms, had impinged on her imagination.

'Oh, well,' Arianna had shrugged. 'He will come round.'

Camilla had decided she wouldn't hold her breath waiting for it to happen. Nic would never appreciate being made a fool of, but that had seemed a risk worth taking in the circumstances. What he would find impossible to forgive, however, was the belief that she had duped him sexually. Used her body as bait as she got him to confide in her about his relationship with Rachelle.

He opened the door to me on his private nightmare, she thought desolately. He'll hate me for that.

Once, in those first hopeful days, she'd seen *Calliope* in the bay, under sail, and had thought for a few heart-stopping moments that she was heading for the sea house, only to watch the caique's tan sail disappear round the headland, and out of sight.

She wondered if she would manage to find the emotional strength to come back for the wedding, once the break with Karthos had been made. Maybe by then she'd have pulled her life together—stopped hurting quite so much, she thought. Although that would largely depend on whether or not she was expecting Nic's baby, she reminded herself unhappily.

She looked at herself in the mirror, noting almost objectively her shadowed eyes and the hollows beneath her cheekbones.

No doubt about it, Dryden, you're an all-round mess, she told herself.

The sudden bang of the main door made her jump. She heard the click of heels across the tiles, then the door of her room crashed open and Arianna stood there, dishevelled and out of breath.

'Camilla.' Her voice was almost hysterical. 'You must help me—save me from Nicos.'

And she burst into tears.

'What are you talking about?' Camilla looked past her, half expecting to see a vengeful Nic close on her heels.

'Nicos came back from Athens an hour ago—perhaps more,' Arianna vouchsafed between sobs. 'He was quiet—strange. He sent for me—told me that when Katie goes to the Peloponnese I must accompany her—and stay there with our aunts until my own marriage has been arranged.'

Her pretty face was haggard. 'I argued with him—but he would not listen. And I shall die in the Peloponnese. Indeed, I would rather be dead than marry some stranger he has chosen for me.'

Camilla groaned inwardly. 'You know you don't mean that.'

'I do. Without Petros, my life is nothing. And Nicos means to send him away—to ruin him for disobeying his wishes over Spiro.'

'I'm sure he didn't mean that.'

Somehow, Camilla got the near-hysterical girl into the kitchen and coaxed her to drink some coffee.

'You don't know,' Arianna said, blotting her face with a handful of tissues. 'Nicos is hard—like a rock—like ice.' She looked pleadingly at Camilla. 'So you will help us, *ne*?'

'I think I'm the last person your brother would listen to,' Camilla said with a sigh.

'Not that—not talking,' Arianna said impatiently. 'I want to leave Karthos—to go to England with you, Camilla. Later, Petros can come for me there, and we will be married. And I will never see my brother again.'

Camilla put her cup down with care. 'I don't believe you've thought this through,' she said. 'For one thing I leave in the morning...'

'I know that.' Arianna tapped her soft leather shoulder-bag. 'I have my passport, also money. No problem.'

'There's the small matter of a seat on the plane,' Camilla reminded her drily.

Arianna gave her a haughty look. 'I am a Xandreou. They will make room for me.'

And I'll be the one left standing on the tarmac, Camilla thought.

'What are your plans if you get to England?' she asked.

'I shall stay with you,' Arianna said promptly. 'You can hide me when Nicos comes to search for me—as he will.'

It sounded like a scenario for a nightmare.

'You realise he'll be worried sick as well as damned angry,' Camilla said curtly. 'You can't treat him like this.' She took a breath. 'Go back and talk to him, Arianna. Tell him how unhappy you are, and why. You may find he understands better than you think. But confrontation won't help, and neither will running away.'

Arianna bounced to her feet. 'You're saying you won't help?'

'It wouldn't be any use to do what you're asking. I'd just make matters worse, and I've done enough of that already.' Camilla kept her voice steady. 'I really think you should go back to the Villa Apollo.'

'Never,' Arianna flared. 'He would lock me in my room until we left for the mainland.'

It occurred to Camilla that Nic might have a point. 'Does he know where you are now?'

'No, of course not,' Arianna said scathingly. 'He will not know I am gone until tomorrow.'

'Then go back the way you came—and sleep on it,' Camilla urged. 'You'll both have calmed down tomorrow, and feel more prepared to be reasonable.'

'*Ochi*.' The Greek girl's face was stormy. 'If you will not help, I make my own way, and to hell for you.'

'With you,' Camilla corrected automatically, and with one last furious glare Arianna whirled out of the kitchen.

Camilla chased after her. 'Where are you going?'

'Away, now—tonight,' the other flung over her shoulder. 'Where no one will find me.'

'Please speak to Nic first,' Camilla appealed. 'Or I will.'

'I don't think so.' Arianna was triumphant. 'There's no telephone here, and you don't have a car. It's a very long walk, I think, and by the time you get there I will be gone—forever.'

'Damnation,' Camilla exploded in frustration as Arianna drove off.

She should have stopped her somehow, and she knew it. Arianna was quite capable of driving to the port and catching the last ferry to Zakynthos, from which there'd be regular flights all over Europe. It would be all too easy for her to disappear.

She felt cold suddenly. Arianna might be spoiled and wilful, but she'd led a sheltered life, and that, coupled with her beauty, made her vulnerable.

I can't just let her vanish into the night, she thought frantically. But I can't follow her either—not on foot, or from the back of beyond.

But she must do something. Nic thought badly enough of her as it was, and nothing could change that, but she couldn't let Arianna charge unhindered down a road to self-destruction.

Whatever Greek men might do with their lives, Camilla had already deduced that the rules which applied to women were very different. And a headlong flight by Xandreou's

sister was just the thing to set malicious tongues
wagging.

If Arianna broke the code, however un-
reasonable it might seem to an outsider, the
Xandreou family pride and prestige could be
damaged, perhaps irrevocably. And Arianna
and Petros would become exiles, with no way
back.

She thought, I can't let it happen.

From the terrace, she could see the lights of
the Villa Apollo shimmering across the silken
calm of the sea. They looked almost close
enough to touch, but she knew that was an
illusion.

But they were within swimming distance. Nic
himself had told her so, a lifetime ago, when
things were still simple between them.

She stood very still for a moment, thinking.
She'd swum regularly in the bay, and never
come across any potentially dangerous cur-
rents there. And there was no breeze tonight.
If she took it steadily, she could make it.

She didn't allow time for second thoughts.
She dragged her one-piece blue swimsuit out
of the case, and put it on. It was the one she
wore to the local baths at home.

I'll pretend that's where I am—seeing how
many lengths I can do, she told herself deter-
minedly, ignoring the nervous flutters in her
stomach.

She left her wrap and sandals at the foot of
the steps, then, taking a deep breath, ran down
to the edge of the sea.

CHAPTER TWELVE

THE water felt chilly against her warm skin. Camilla waded in till it was chest-high, then struck out smoothly, deliberately not hurrying.

It was a totally different experience, somehow, swimming at night. The dark water was mysterious, full of whispers and movement. Once something seemed to brush past her, and she bit back a cry, reminding herself of the shoals of fish she'd swum among in daylight. It could even have been a strand of weed, or just her imagination playing tricks.

As soon as she felt tired, she turned on to her back and floated for a while until she was rested enough to go on. There was a brief sickle of a moon above her now, like a friendly beacon, lighting her way towards her lover— her enemy.

She changed her stroke to a crawl, cutting easily through the water. She seemed to be making real headway now, with the lights from the Villa Apollo appearing much closer at last. She must be well past the point of no return, she thought, her heart jumping nervously.

Don't think about that, she adjured herself. Concentrate on your breathing, and moving your arms and legs correctly to take full advantage of every stroke. Textbook stuff.

But she needed more than theory to get her through tonight. A fair helping of luck wouldn't come amiss, she thought, treading water to get her bearings. This time, to her dismay, her destination seemed as far away as ever. Maybe she was doomed to swim forever, like some ill-fated mermaid, while the Villa Apollo, like Nic himself, stayed always out of reach.

I was crazy to have started this, she thought, suddenly aware of how cold she was getting, how increasingly difficult it was to maintain that first easy rhythm.

But she mustn't think like that. It wasn't just defeatist, but downright dangerous. Somehow she had to go on. The choice was out of her hands.

All the choices had been out of her hands since the moment she'd first set foot on Karthos. She realised that now. She'd been the plaything of fate since day one.

And if she went down into the sea—the wine-dark sea—that would be fate too. And it would be so easy. She felt the drag of the water at her weary limbs. And then remembered what had brought her this far.

Nic, she thought dazedly, pushing her aching body forward. She had to see him—to tell him—something. What exactly didn't seem to matter any more. The important thing was to see him—to hear his voice—to touch him once more before she left—before the old, drab life closed over her head like the sea.

In her head, she seemed to hear him calling her, urging her on. Eyes closed, arms and legs like lead, she concentrated every nerve, every muscle, every scrap of will on survival.

She was hardly aware of the light at first. It was only a faint blur behind her tired eyelids, but with every stroke it seemed to swell and grow until it filled the universe. And there were voices too—men's voices, shouting something.

Her flailing arms brushed something solid—planking, she realised dazedly—then something seized her, held her, pulling her up into the light.

She cried out in fright, and pain as her muscles protested. When she opened her eyes, she found herself lying on *Calliope*'s deck, with Nic bending over her.

She barely recognised him. His face was grey, his voice hoarse. 'What have you done?' he demanded. 'In the name of God, why are you here? Are you insane?'

She wanted to put up a hand and smooth away the haggard lines beside his mouth, the crease between his brows. Her heart cried out, I love you. Her mouth tried to form the words.

From a great distance she heard her voice, husky and laboured, say, 'Arianna's run away. You—you must stop her.' Then she fainted.

She was in the sea again, the water lapping round her, loading her down, enclosing her so that she couldn't breathe—and she was struggling, fighting her way to the surface.

'Be still, *pedhi mou*. You are safe now.'

She forced open her weighted lids, and looked up into Nic's grave face. She was lying in a bed, she realised, with blankets wrapped round her, swaddling her. That was why she'd felt she couldn't move.

'You have to rest—keep warm,' he said quietly. 'Petros's orders must be obeyed.'

'Petros?' Camilla frowned as memory began to nudge at her. 'Is he here? But surely...'

'He is downstairs with Arianna.' He paused for a moment. 'After she left you, she went to him, it seems, and he brought her back.'

'Oh, thank God.' Camilla felt sudden tears scalding her eyes. 'Please—don't be angry with her. She's so unhappy.'

'Indeed?' The dark brows lifted quizzically. 'When I saw her last, she was smiling and drinking champagne in celebration of her engagement.'

'Engagement?' Camilla ran her tongue round her dry lips.

'To Petros, naturally.' Nic's gaze bored into her. 'Or did you think I was blind to what was going on?'

'But she said you had plans for her—an arranged marriage.'

He shrugged. 'I was testing her,' he said flatly. 'I wanted to discover if she really loved Petros, or was simply enjoying the drama of a secret romance. He is too good—as a man, and as a friend—to be at the mercy of her whims and fancies, if she had no serious intentions towards him.' He smiled faintly. 'But as she was prepared to abandon everything for a hand-to-mouth existence with him on the other side of Europe, I had to believe her sincerity.'

He sighed. 'I only hope he knows what he is taking on,' he added drily. His smile became slightly crooked. 'So true love triumphs over circumstances again, Camilla. You should be delighted. Another victory for you.'

'I had nothing to do with it,' she protested, suddenly and uncomfortably aware that she was naked inside the cocoon of blankets. 'But I'm glad that everything's worked out for them,' she added rather stiltedly. 'Even if I did make that swim for nothing.'

'Ah, yes,' he said softly. 'That swim.' He paused, and Camilla felt tension crackle in the air. 'You crazy little fool. Don't you know you could have drowned?'

She forced a smile to trembling lips. 'It did occur to me—several times. But I had to tell you—to warn you what Arianna intended.'

There was a silence, then he said, 'Was that the only reason?'

She felt a wave of betraying warmth sweep over her. 'There was no other way to reach you,' she prevaricated.

Nic shook his head. 'That was not what I asked, *matia mou*, and you know it.'

She said in a little rush, 'I couldn't bear to see you hurt again. I knew if Arianna talked to you, told you how she felt, you'd understand.'

'You had more faith in me than she did,' he said with a touch of grimness.

She didn't look at him. 'Perhaps you don't see things too clearly when you're in love,' she said in a low voice.

'No.' His voice was reflective. 'So—it was just for Arianna's sake that you chose to risk your life?'

She picked at the edging of a blanket. 'Not—totally.'

'So?'

She sighed. 'I didn't want to leave—with all this misunderstanding between us.'

'Tell me something.' Nic's fingers closed round her chin, tilting it so that he could study her flushed face. 'When you came with me to Marynthos—and afterwards—was it only so that your sister could meet with Spiro?'

'No,' she said. 'At least—I wouldn't have pushed myself on to you as I did—but if you'd asked me I'd have gone with you.' She stopped, confused and miserable. 'You were right all along, you see. I was—yours for the taking, only I didn't want to admit it.' Her little laugh cracked in the middle. 'Just another of Xandreou's women after all.'

'You flatter me,' he said with irony. He released her. 'I'll carve another notch on the bedhead, and we'll part friends. Is that what you want?'

What I want? she could have shrieked at him. Body, heart and soul, I ache—burn for you.

She said, 'I—hope we can be friends, certainly. Maybe one day you'll come to see that Katie and Spiro are happy together, and that the end has justified the means.'

'You thought I was angry because I'd been made a fool of,' he said. 'But that was only part of it. I was frightened, Camilla. Scared that when Spiro regained his memory I might lose him.' He sat for a moment, looking down at his hands, his face brooding.

'We quarrelled, you see, before the accident,' he went on. 'I said cruel things—damaging things about your sister. Made assumptions that he resented. I have never seen him so angry—so determined. He said he was going to her, and there was nothing I could do to stop him. That if his marriage to her meant a complete breach between us, then that was how it would be.'

He shook his head. 'We were both furious—emotional. I knew he was driving to the ferry—I should have stopped him—calmed him down. He wasn't fit to be in charge of a car, and I knew it. But—I let him go.' His voice broke. 'When I saw the car, crumpled against a tree, Spiro slumped over the wheel, I knew I could never forgive myself.'

His voice sank almost to a whisper. 'I feared that when Spiro remembered it would only be the anger—the bitterness. Both he and Arianna—I have had to be responsible for them for so long—more like their father than their brother. I suppose I wanted to protect them both—too much.'

'I felt the same with Katie,' Camilla confessed. 'I wasn't overjoyed when she first told me about Spiro, believe me.'

He smiled faintly. 'I do, *pedhi mou*. We both—underestimated them perhaps.' He threw his head back. 'I came to realise that while Spiro had that blank in his memory he belonged to me—depended on me again, and I was disgusted at my own selfishness—my own cowardice.'

'But in reality you had nothing to fear,' Camilla said softly.

'No,' he admitted. 'Spiro has been—generous. Your sister also.' He reached out and took her hand, staring at her fingers as if he was committing them to memory. 'If I had chosen her myself, I could have found no better match for him. I—see that now.'

She bit her lip, feeling tears sting at her eyes. 'You can be generous too, Kyrios Xandreou.'

'I need to make amends, Kyria Dryden.' His mouth smiled at their formality, but the dark eyes were serious.

'And now it's my turn.' She swallowed. 'I did agree to keep you out of the way that day, but only because I felt I had no choice. I felt such a fraud when your friends were so nice to me. I found I wanted the day to be real, with no pretence—no hidden agenda.'

'And it was real?' His voice was harsh suddenly. 'When we were together, a man and a woman with nothing but our need for each other? Or was it more pretence—and pity?'

'Pity?' she echoed in shock. 'Oh, God, do you really think I could have behaved like that—given myself to you—because I thought you'd had a raw deal with your marriage?' She shook her head. 'You don't know me very well.'

'And that is something I mean to change.' He put her hand against his mouth, his lips grazing her skin, sending a shiver of sensuous yearning through her body. 'Where do you think I was going in *Calliope* tonight, *agape mou*, when I pulled you from the sea?'

'Going?' She frowned. 'I don't know.'

'No?' He smiled at her, a tenderness in his face that she had never seen before. 'To the sea house, my Camilla. To ask you to stay—on my knees, if I had to.'

She said with a catch in her voice, 'I thought you went to Athens to get away from me.'

He grimaced. 'So did I. But you've been with me every moment of this endless, damnable week, invading my thoughts all day, torturing my dreams at night in spite of myself.'

She looked at him under her lashes, swiftly and shyly. 'In spite of Zoe too?'

Nic looked resigned. 'My beloved sister, no doubt. I shall instruct Petros to beat her regularly when they are married. Yes, my sweet devil, in spite of Zoe, who found me poor company on the one occasion I took her to dinner. However, I don't know which of us was more surprised when I suddenly heard myself telling her I would not be seeing her again.

'That moment was like a catalyst. I knew then what I had been fighting so desperately to deny.' He framed her face very gently in his hands. 'That I love you, *matia mou*, my sweet girl who gave me the innocence in her eyes.'

Camilla said with a little sob, 'Oh, Nic.'

'Hear me out, *agape mou*. When Spiro called me to say you planned to leave tomorrow, I cancelled my meetings and flew back. I could not let things rest as they were between us. I had to see you—to tell you what was in my heart—to ask you if we could cancel out the unkindness, the mistrust, and begin again.'

He smoothed back a strand of still damp hair from her forehead. 'I also need to know, my dear one, if you can love me.'

She smiled at him, eyes shining, lips tremulous. 'I lost my battle long ago, *kyrie*. Why else would I swim further than I've ever done in my life, if not to be with you?'

He was very still for a moment, then with a groan he lay beside her, gathering her into his arms as carefully as if she were made of spun glass, planting swift, sweet kisses on her hair, forehead and eyes.

'I really knew,' he told her softly, 'that day when I saw you with Hara's baby in your arms. It came to me, like a bolt of thunder, how much I wished to see you holding our child.'

'That's a wish that might be granted sooner than you think,' Camilla said ruefully.

'The possibility troubles you?'

'No.' She shook her head. 'But I'd better cut out the strenuous exercise from now on, just in case.'

'Yes,' he said grimly. 'You will. Dear God.' He smothered a groan. 'How easily I could have lost you.'

'Never.' She was laughing now, warmly, glowingly provocative as she eased herself out of the encircling blankets and watched the answering fire kindle in his dark eyes. 'Darling Nic, it was all fate. I was born to be Xandreou's woman.'

'No, *sigismos mou*,' he said softly as he bent to her, mouth and hands sensuous against her skin, drawing her against the vibrant beat of his heart. 'Xandreou's wife.'

BRIDE'S BAY RESORT

UNLOCK THE DOOR TO GREAT ROMANCE AT BRIDE'S BAY RESORT

Join Harlequin's new across-the-lines series, set in an exclusive hotel on an island off the coast of South Carolina.

Seven of your favorite authors will bring you exciting stories about fascinating heroes and heroines discovering love at Bride's Bay Resort.

Look for these fabulous stories coming to a store near you beginning in January 1996.

Harlequin American Romance #613 in January
Matchmaking Baby by Cathy Gillen Thacker

Harlequin Presents #1794 in February
Indiscretions by Robyn Donald

Harlequin Intrigue #362 in March
Love and Lies by Dawn Stewardson

Harlequin Romance #3404 in April
Make Believe Engagement by Day Leclaire

Harlequin Temptation #588 in May
Stranger in the Night by Roseanne Williams

Harlequin Superromance #695 in June
Married to a Stranger by Connie Bennett

Harlequin Historicals #324 in July
Dulcie's Gift by Ruth Langan

Visit Bride's Bay Resort each month wherever Harlequin books are sold.

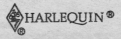

HARLEQUIN ®

BBAYG

Take 4 bestselling love stories FREE

Plus get a FREE surprise gift!

Special Limited-time Offer

Mail to Harlequin Reader Service®

3010 Walden Avenue
P.O. Box 1867
Buffalo, N.Y. 14269-1867

YES! Please send me 4 free Harlequin Presents® novels and my free surprise gift. Then send me 6 brand-new novels every month, which I will receive months before they appear in bookstores. Bill me at the low price of $2.66 each plus 25¢ delivery and applicable sales tax, if any*. That's the complete price and a savings of over 10% off the cover prices—quite a bargain! I understand that accepting the books and gift places me under no obligation ever to buy any books. I can always return a shipment and cancel at any time. Even if I never buy another book from Harlequin, the 4 free books and the surprise gift are mine to keep forever.

106 BPA AW6U

Name	(PLEASE PRINT)	
Address		Apt. No.
City	State	Zip

This offer is limited to one order per household and not valid to present Harlequin Presents® subscribers. *Terms and prices are subject to change without notice. Sales tax applicable in N.Y.

UPRES-995   ©1990 Harlequin Enterprises Limited

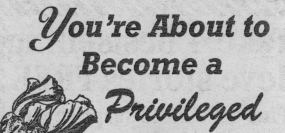

You're About to Become a *Privileged Woman*

Reap the rewards of fabulous free gifts and benefits with proofs-of-purchase from Harlequin and Silhouette books

Pages & Privileges™

It's our way of thanking you for buying our books at your favorite retail stores.

PROOF OF PURCHASE
HP-PP95
Offer expires October 31, 1996

Pages & Privileges™

Harlequin and Silhouette—
the most privileged readers in the world!

For more information about Harlequin and Silhouette's PAGES & PRIVILEGES program call the Pages & Privileges Benefits Desk: **1-503-794-2499**

HARLEQUIN®

HP-PP95